All
Hallows'
Shadows

Also by Michael D. Graves

To Leave a Shadow

A 2016 Kansas Notable Book

Shadow of Death

Green Bike, a group novel
with Kevin Rabas and Tracy Million Simmons

All Hallows' Shadows

by Michael D. Graves

Meadowlark PRESS

Emporia, Kansas, USA

Meadowlark
Meadowlark-books.com
Emporia, Kansas

Cover photo by Dave Leiker
daveleikerphotography.com

ISBN: 978-1-7342477-3-2

Library of Congress Control Number: 2020932326

0209202TMS

In Memory of
Bill Lang

"Though this be madness,

yet there is method in't."

Hamlet

Grandma was Special

Grandma was Special

Even before she told me her story about seeing the ghost of her great uncle, I knew my grandma was special. She possessed a quiet patience, a dignity sometimes lacking in others. When a crisis arose, when others flitted and flew and squandered time and energy on futile gestures, Grandma waited and observed. She bided her time, thoughtful and calm. She peered into corners and gazed into shadows. Grandma noticed things that other people missed.

"It was cold that night, cold and clear and still. An early frost hung in the air, and I tucked the blanket up under my chin. Full moon shining. What was it Papa said? A dying grass moon, he called it. That was it. A dying grass moon, that full October moon. Trees going bare, long shadows, no stars. Some claimed that spirits stirred on such a night. An owl hooted. A twig snapped. I started, my little girl imagination turning to ghosts and goblins and such. A body felt mighty small beneath that prairie sky."

"Were you scared, Grandma?"

"Oh, no, not really, not with Papa on one side and Momma on the other. I was safe. Our mare snorted and snuffed and leaned into the harness, blowing clouds of mist. The buggy creaked and rattled. I curled beneath the blanket and snuggled close to Momma. She slept on the seat, and her jowls jiggled as we passed over the rutted road. Papa dozed on my other side, reins loose over one hand. He'd snuck out behind the barn to tip a jug between dances, him and his pals, thinking the ladies would be none the wiser, and the ladies pretended they didn't notice. Corn liquor had lifted his spirits and claimed his body. He fought sleep. His head bobbed and dropped, down, down, then snapped up like a fish hooked on a line. He popped open his eyes, twisted his neck, puffed his cheeks and blew a breath. He gazed into the darkness, got his bearings and did it all over again. His eyelids drooped, his head bobbed, his chin dropped. I tried not to giggle. I wondered why he just didn't go to sleep. That mare knew the way home as well as Papa did, and she didn't need any prodding to get there neither."

Grandma's chuckle spilled over her pink gums, and her tongue flicked over her lips. Her teary eyes squinted behind the tiny wire-framed glasses that rested on her nose. Light from a dim bulb ha-loed the white bun atop her head. She looked angelic.

"What about the ghost, Grandma? When did you see the ghost?"

"Well, as we drew near our place the road rose up over a nar-row bridge that passed over a creek. That was our guidepost, our signal that home was just ahead, that bridge. The mare knew it, too, and she leaned forward and stepped a bit faster. That's when I saw him, just out of the shadows, standing right there on that bridge in the light of the moon. I saw a tall man, a thin man, what we called gaunt. He wore long gray whiskers, and he had a black top hat. Under a dark coat he wore a red checkered vest with a gold chain draped across it."

"Wow, a real ghost! Now were you scared?"

Grandma smiled and gathered me in with fleshy arms and dimpled elbows and laid my head against her breast. She patted my head and whispered.

"No, child, no I wasn't afraid, not in the least. I grew rather calm. I saw no reason to be afraid, no reason at all. The man smiled at me and raised a hand and waved and nodded as we rolled by, and then he faded back into the shadows."

"And you didn't even know who it was?"

"Not then, I didn't, no. The next morning at breakfast, I told about what I'd seen. When I described the man, my folks stopped chewing their food. They put down their forks and listened. And when I told about the red checkered vest and gold chain, Momma gave Papa a look. Neither one spoke. I said, 'What? What is it?' and Momma took my hand and said, 'That was the spirit of your great uncle, Horace, dear. That's just what he looked like, tall and gaunt with a long beard. He was so proud of that watch and chain, a wedding gift from his bride. He bought a red vest to better show it off and never went anywhere without it.'

"I asked Momma when he had died, and she said, 'Before you were born. He died not long after his wife passed over. She went with rheumatic fever, and her death left him heartbroken. He took to drinking. Some say his horse threw him that night. Others say he simply fell out of the saddle after an evening spent with John Barleycorn. Either way, he died right there, right at that bridge. They found his body in the creek.'"

A chill fell over me.

"Wow. So, you really did see a ghost, huh, Grandma? You really did?"

"Yes, I did. My mother said I had a gift, what with being born on Easter Sunday and all, but I don't know. Seeing a ghost never seemed all that unusual to me. It seemed perfectly normal. I never have believed that we're alone in this life. I figure that anyone who's willing to slow down a bit, to tread easy, to look into the shadows—those folks will discover magic, magic that busy folks might miss."

"What kind of magic, Grandma?"

Grandma chuckled.

"You just wait, little one. Just wait and watch. Slow down. Go easy. You'll see."

She hugged me, and I wanted to speak, but I was interrupted by a bell, a harsh clanging sound, over and over.

"What's that sound, Grandma, that ringing? What's that noise?"

She smiled and opened her arms and released me. She fell away, grew faint and faded into the shadows. The clanging grew louder and repeated, again and again, jangles that didn't stop, wouldn't stop.

"Grandma, where are you? Don't leave. Come back," but she was gone. I could no longer see her.

My eyes opened, and I lay still. The ringing continued. From where? I grabbed the alarm clock on the nightstand, but it was silent. The ringing came from a distance. I tossed back the blanket and threw my legs over the side of the bed. My feet got tangled in the sheets, and I tripped and cracked my shin on the nightstand. I cursed the pain and hobbled to the kitchen. The telephone sat on the table alongside an ashtray and a pack of Chesterfields. I reached for the telephone with one hand and the cigarettes with the other.

"Yes, hello?" I said into the receiver. I shook a cigarette from the pack, and a masculine voice came over the line.

"Good morning. Is this Mr. Stone? Am I speaking to Mr. Pete Stone?"

My reply was interrupted by another sound of bells, bells tinkling in tune along with gongs and chimes, in chorus with cuckoos and chirps. Unlike the harsh clangs of the telephone, however, these lullabies greeted me each morning and eased me to sleep each night. My collection of clocks heralded the hours, the Black Forest cuckoo clock, the Seth Thomas grandfather clock, the recently acquired Austrian Zappler Animated clock, and over a dozen others scattered throughout the house. The owner of the voice on the other end of the line heard the chimes, too, and was wise enough to hold his tongue until they ceased. I used the respite to cradle the phone on my shoulder and hold a match to a cigarette. Each clock sounded nine times in unison. I prided myself on their accuracy. When they ceased their recital, the voice spoke again. It sounded impatient.

"Well, finally. Please tell me, have I reached Mr. Pete Stone?"

"Yes, you have and a good morning to you, sir."

I saw no reason to be unpleasant. The day had just begun. It still held promise, and I still had hope. My sunny tone must have caught the speaker off guard. There was a pause. Then he continued.

"Mr. Stone, my name is Fallon, Dr. Wilfred Fallon, and I am a professor of English at Wichita University. I'm calling you because you have been recommended to me. That is, someone I trust suggested that I give you a call."

He cleared his throat and continued.

"Please forgive me for ringing you at home, Mr. Stone, but I tried your office, and your secretary said you hadn't arrived yet. It is now nine o'clock in the morning. May I ask what time you usually begin your day?"

"You may ask," I said, "but my answer is none of your business."

I rethought my earlier decision to remain pleasant.

"Of course, you're correct. Forgive me, please. Your personal schedule is none of my business. Maybe I should start again. I'm afraid I've been under a bit of a strain lately, and I haven't been myself. It's been some time since I've been so baffled by circumstances and so unsure about how to proceed. That's why I called. As I mentioned, you come recommended to me by someone I admire and respect. I'm calling to inquire into the particulars of engaging your services."

I mulled over the caller's priggish vocabulary. Most of my clients just hired me. No one in memory had ever inquired into the particulars of engaging my services.

"What's this about, Professor Fallon?"

"I'm not sure how to begin. Are you familiar with the murder of a recent university graduate? It's been in the papers."

I assured Fallon that I had read about the crime.

"I read the papers," I said. "According to the reports, a young woman was stabbed, and a suspect was caught soon after the body was discovered. The case hasn't gone to trial, but the police are confident they have the guilty party in custody. It appears to be open and shut."

"Yes, that's right," the professor said, "that was the report. At least that's the report that was issued to the public. However, I have doubts about the case being open and shut, as you succinctly put it. I think the police may have arrested the wrong man. I believe that the suspect the police have in custody is innocent. I'd like to hire you to investigate the matter on your own, to conduct a more thorough examination. As you say, the police are confident their suspect is guilty. I do not share their confidence. Not at all. I'd like to hire you to find the real murderer."

I glanced at the empty coffeepot on the stove. On a normal day, I consumed at least three cups of hot, black joe before speaking to a soul, let alone a faceless voice over the telephone.

"Dr. Fallon, this is a police matter. You should be talking to them. If you have proof or information regarding the suspect's innocence, you should go to the police immediately."

"No, please understand. I do not have proof, and I cannot go to the police. I do have doubts, serious doubts, and I'd like to discuss them with you."

"Even so, even with no proof, if you know anything about this case that the police don't know, you should go to them."

I waited for a reply.

"Mr. Stone, I cannot go to the police for reasons I do not wish to divulge over the phone. If we met together our discussion might prove more enlightening and fruitful. Would you be willing to meet with me?"

I questioned in my mind if Fallon knew something about the murder that had escaped the police's attention. It seemed doubtful. The newspaper reports suggested the police had arrested the murderer.

"To tell you the truth, professor, I'd planned on taking a few days off this week."

Fallon was not put off by my comment.

"May I suggest this?" he said. "Give me an hour here in my office. One hour. I will pay you for your time and trouble whether you choose to assist me or not. Would that be agreeable?"

He was determined and anxious. Why was he reluctant to talk to the police? His request to meet him seemed reasonable, and I had to admit that he had piqued my curiosity.

"Okay, professor," I said. "I suppose an hour together couldn't hurt."

"Excellent. How about this morning, before lunch? Say eleven-thirty?"

I assured him that would be fine, and he told me where to find him on campus. We said our good-byes and rang off. I went to the stove and started a pot of coffee and showered and dressed while it brewed. After I finished knotting my tie, I poured a cup of coffee and dialed my secretary, Agnes, at my office. I took my first sip of the hot liquid just as she answered my ring with, "Pete Stone Investigations."

"Good morning, my sweet Dulcinea. This is your Don Quixote calling, your knight errant, incurable romantic, tilter at windmills, and righter of wrongs."

"Well, the day is young," Agnes said, "but you sound like you're already into the sauce. Are you starting early, or have you been nursing your habit all night long?"

"Wrong on both counts, sister, and I'm offended at your insinuations. As a matter of fact, all I'm nursing is coffee, straight and black. I'm as sober as a schoolmarm, and I'm perpendicular to the world, thank you very much. It's early in the ballgame, but I'm batting two for two."

"First, you're Don Quixote, and now you're Babe Ruth. If either one of you hear from Pete Stone, you might ask him to give me a call. I'd like to hear how things went last night."

"Pete Stone is alive and well, kiddo. Thanks for asking. The hooligans are in the hoosegow, viewing the world from behind cell bars. Thanks to yours truly, the streets of our Peerless Princess of the Plains are safer this day than they were the day before."

Agnes was referring to my most recent case. I had spent the previous evening and several of the wee hours that morning on a stakeout involving a break-in and stolen goods. Two recent graduates of the Kansas State Penitentiary at Lansing had celebrated their release by boosting a truck from a warehouse near Second and Wabash. I had done some work for the owner of the warehouse in the past with satisfactory results. Although I suspected that not every item of his inventory would pass muster under the eyes of the law, I was a private investigator, not a judge. When he told me that the truck in question carried a load of crates marked "Carnation Milk," he offered a nod and a wink. So, it wasn't really milk in the crates. It was no skin off my nose. Like I mentioned, who was I to judge? When I worked for him earlier, we'd both been pleased with the outcome, so I didn't ask unnecessary questions. I accepted the job.

The thieves left a trail that three blind mice could follow. I tracked them to a neighborhood near Lewis and Laura that had an auto repair shop on the corner and a welding shop next door.

Across the street was a brief row of frame houses, two white and one gray. The stolen truck was parked in the driveway of the gray house. A tall sycamore tree with leaves gone yellow stood sentinel in front.

What the two culprits lacked in smarts they made up for in enthusiasm. I peeked through a window and caught them throwing a party for themselves and a half-dozen scantily clad ladies of the night. No other males were in sight. I didn't fault their ambitiousness. Maybe the ladies had a group rate.

A portable Victrola phonograph rested on a table in one corner of the living room and played the mellow notes of Bing Crosby's, "Just One More Chance." The tune seemed prophetic. Maybe that's what the men were looking for, just one more chance. Several bottles of liquor were arrayed on a sideboard, no doubt liberated from the crates marked as milk. The two men took turns dancing with the women. Everyone held a drink.

I almost hated to break up the party, a couple of horny, drunk ex-cons blowing off a little steam. If I went in, there'd be screaming and shouting and violence, and who knew who'd get hurt. There might even be gunplay. None of that sounded good. So, I decided to be patient, to bide my time and let the celebration wind down on its own.

I returned to my roadster parked on the street a couple of doors down and waited and watched. The scent of new mown grass wafted in the air. The scent and the season turned my thoughts to baseball. I mulled over the upcoming World Series and wondered if the Yankees would take it again this year or if the Giants might figure out a way to topple them. The Yankees had Lefty Gomez on the mound, but the Giants countered with Carl Hubbell, neither one a slouch. Still, the smart money was on the Yankees.

The night wore on, and I listened to noises in the dark. A dog barked. A cat meowed. A screen door slammed. My thoughts drifted from baseball to women, from loves to losses, and finally to one woman, a woman who was not yet a love and not yet a loss. A woman who would be easy to love if she would let me. So far, she hadn't. She had been betrayed by a man she trusted and had grown cautious, maybe too cautious. We were attracted to each other, but she'd shied from my advances, and I had backed off. At first, I was hurt by her rebuffs, but I came to understand. I, too, had known betrayal.

I had once fallen for an angel who turned out to be a succubus in disguise. I fell for her charms like the clown who slips on a banana peel. She pretended to love me when all she truly loved was money, and she proved she was willing to do anything to get it. When I discovered her deceit, our relationship ended. Badly.

From that moment on, I promised to myself, I would be more careful and move slowly. Part of me promised, anyway. Not all of me did. Cautiousness had its place, but it seldom led to romance, and right then, my romantic prospects looked darker than the midnight sky.

My watch ticked away the minutes, and the accumulation of cigarette butts on the street outside my roadster grew larger. I smoked and waited. Much of my work involved waiting. The party finally quieted down. The music stopped, and the lights in the gray house dimmed. The door opened, and several of the women staggered onto the porch and disappeared into the night. A couple of women remained in the house.

An owl hooted. I waited a while longer, then I opened the car door and eased out onto the street. I stretched my stiff legs and back and strolled to the phone booth on the corner. I placed two calls, the first an anonymous tip to the police, the second to the owner of the stolen goods.

By the time the police arrived, the thieves were passed out cold. They came awake with only a vague sense of where they were and what they'd done. The men in blue subdued them with little trouble and no violence. The two remaining women were questioned briefly and released back into the shadows. The warehouse owner arrived in a sedan with another guy in the passenger seat. He explained to the police that the "milk" on the truck was to be delivered to a hospital in Topeka later that morning. The cops took the owner's statement while the other guy climbed into the truck and rolled away. A few minutes later, the warehouse owner got back in his car. He gave me the high sign as he drove by. I gave him a nod and drove home under a gray sky going pink. My head hit the pillow just as the sun peeked over the horizon.

"All is well," I said to Agnes. "The culprits have been apprehended and are in police custody. The case is closed."

"Good for you," Agnes said.

"And no shots were fired."

"Always a good thing," she said.

"Always a good thing," I said.

"A call came in this morning," Agnes said, "from a professor at the university."

"I know. He just called me. He's the reason I'm up at this unkind hour."

"Oh, Pete, I'm sorry. I didn't give him your home number."

"I know you didn't, sweetheart. Don't worry about it. I got a couple of hours of shuteye. A good night's sleep is overrated. I'll be fine, as soon as I've had another cup of plasma. Then I'm off to see the professor."

We chatted a bit longer about this, that, and the other thing and rang off. I drank more coffee and smoked another cigarette for breakfast, tidied up the kitchen, and headed out the door bound for the university. I closed the door at my place just as the chimes and gongs began their eleven o'clock serenade.

Little Did I Know

T he Municipal University lay in the northeast part of Wichita across town from my place on Lewellen Street. I drove north a couple of blocks and noticed homes decorated in orange and black, early birds ready for Halloween. When I came to the high school, I turned east on Thirteenth. Late morning traffic was light, and I made good time. The weather was on its best behavior, as fall weather often is in Kansas. The buffeting southerly winds had abated as had the summer's searing temperatures. Clear skies beckoned and gave a soul promise. I drove with the top down on my Jones Six roadster and breathed the crisp autumn air.

October was my favorite month. I'd told the truth to the professor about my intention to knock off for a few days. My plans involved baseball and beer, and I'd earned a break. The World Series was scheduled to open in two days, and my pal Tom would have his Motorola tuned in to the games and a stool reserved for me at the tavern bearing his name. Red Barber and his cronies would woo me with their play-by-play. I'd smoke stogies and kibitz with Tom, dine on peanuts and hotdogs, and quaff mugs of Storz beer until the final pitch signaled the end of the fall classic and the onset of the dark season, those soulless months with no baseball.

I reached Hillside and turned north toward the university. At Seventeenth, I went two blocks east to Fairmount and drove onto the campus. I had a few minutes to spare, so I rolled across campus and admired the architecture and landscaping. Trees had turned scarlet and yellow, and golden mums bloomed in well-tended flowerbeds.

The Administration Building, an imposing redbrick structure not unlike other administration buildings, greeted students and visitors. Morrison Library, where my son had spent much of his time as a student and graduate assistant, boasted columns reminiscent of the Parthenon. A new Auditorium and Commons Building was the university's most recent addition, a welcome gathering place for students. Many of them entered and exited, smiling and chatting together. I had read that the university president, W.M. Jardine, took pride in the recent addition, and I could understand why.

The semester was fresh and alive. Students wore expressions of hope and optimism. Final exams loomed a lifetime away. The youthful enthusiasm was contagious, and I confessed to myself that the World Series wasn't all I looked forward to that week. I also intended to call on a certain lady, the widow Lucille Hamilton.

I found myself feeling younger, whistling a tune and tapping my fingers on the steering wheel. I pulled up in front of the Liberal Arts Building and parked next to a late model tan Hudson. I hopped out of my car and strolled up the walkway with a bounce in my step and a grin on my mug. I reached the door just as a coed approached. She greeted me with a warm, toothy smile, and I returned it. The young lady reached ahead of me for the door handle.

"Here you are, sir," she said. "I'd better get that for you."

Her smile beamed. Mine faded. She pulled the door open and stepped aside to allow me passage. So much for the warm spark of youth, I thought.

"Thank you," I said and touched the brim of my hat. Did I look that feeble? I tried not to hobble and somehow managed to get through the doorway.

Inside, students strolled together down the hallway, chatting and laughing and calling out to each other. I passed down the corridor to Room 113 and knocked on the door. A booming voice invited me in. The office hadn't changed since the last time I was there. Papers and books rested in uneven stacks on a desk and several chairs. An array of textbooks and other volumes cluttered the bookshelves, and dust and smoke cast a haze in the air. The overhead light was off, but sunlight filtered through the blinds on a window situated behind the large man seated at the desk.

"Pete Stone! Come in, come in! By Jove, it's good to see you again. Sit down. That's the stuff. Share one of your adventures with a cloistered old history professor. Tell me about the world beyond these ivied walls. Too much of my life is drawn from the pages of a book. Talk to me about real life, life on the street."

I crossed the floor and shook hands with the man seated in a wheelchair behind the desk.

"Hello, Ethan," I said. "It's good to see you again. How have you been?"

"Fine, fine," he said. "You know how history is. It simply repeats itself. Nothing ever changes." He gestured toward a chair. "Go ahead. Sit."

I glanced at my watch and took a seat in the only chair not covered with papers.

"I'm sorry, but I only have time to say hello, Ethan. I have an appointment upstairs, but I wanted to pop in and see you first."

The large man furrowed his brow and drew on his pipe. Ethan Alexander, professor of history, was my son's former teacher and mentor. The wheelchair he sat in was a souvenir he brought home from the Great War some two decades earlier. Rather than live in bitterness over the injuries he suffered, he turned his experience into a quest to learn and understand history and war and the national leaders who started them. As a history professor he shared the results of his learning through the books he wrote and the lectures he gave in the classroom. I had met him when working on a previous case. He had been helpful, and we had developed a mutual fondness and a friendship toward one another. It was good to see him again, if only for a few minutes.

"Ah, yes," he said. "I suppose you're here to meet with Wil Fallon."

I had suspected that Ethan Alexander had referred me to Fallon.

"Yes, he called me this morning and asked me to meet him in his office. He also said I came highly recommended. Thank you, Ethan. I appreciate that."

He brushed aside my thanks with a wave of his pipe.

"Don't thank me, yet. I'm not sure about what you're getting into. Frankly, I don't think Fallon knows, either. Anyway, I wish you good luck. I won't keep you if you have an appointment. Say hello to Wil for me and stop in again before you leave. Don't worry. I won't ask prying questions. It's always good to see you."

"And you, Ethan."

We shook hands again, and I left his office. I climbed the stairs to the second floor, Room 205. The door opened on my knock, and a slight, elderly man ushered me in and closed the door. Instead of taking a seat or offering me one, he paced the floor, his hands clasped behind his back. He stopped beside his desk and turned to me.

"Have you spoken to anyone else?" he said.

"I stopped in to say hello to Ethan Alexander," I said. "He sends his regards." It didn't seem necessary to mention my encounter with the coed at the door.

The man stared at a spot on the floor and nodded.

"That's fine."

He looked up at me and seemed puzzled as to why I was standing in his office.

"Forgive me," he said. "I haven't introduced myself. I'm Wilfred Fallon."

He extended his hand, and I shook it.

"I assume you are Mr. Pete Stone, the man I spoke to on the telephone?"

"That's right."

He gestured toward a chair in front of his desk. I sat down, and he took his chair behind the desk. Fallon's office was furnished much like Alexander's with a desk, straight-backed chairs, and bookshelves, but the similarities ended there. Fallon's office was as neat and organized as Alexander's was cluttered and in disarray. Books lined the shelves in an orderly fashion. Papers on the desk, student essays it appeared, were arranged in a tidy stack. A Tiffany reading lamp stood next to the papers. A book lay near one corner of the desk, a copy of *Modern American Poetry and Modern British Poetry*, edited by Louis Untermeyer. I recognized the book because I owned a copy, a gift from my son, Dan. Fallon's copy appeared to be worn more than my own. Next to the desk was a smaller table with a typewriter resting atop it.

A bust of William Shakespeare perched on a pedestal in a corner of the office. A small fan hummed on a side table and kept the air circulated and fresh. I smelled no tobacco and saw no ashtrays and decided it would be a faux pas to light a cigarette in the room.

The dapper Professor Fallon wore a gray worsted wool suit with vest over a linen shirt and a red silk tie sporting a perfect Windsor knot. A gold chain lay across his vest and disappeared into a pocket, presumably with a watch attached to its end. I chilled at the recollection of the ghost wearing a pocket watch in my dream hours earlier. Fallon's chain matched both the wedding ring on the appropriate finger and the wire spectacles resting on his nose.

Dark eyes, bright and alert, gazed out from behind the spectacles. Not a snowy hair on his head was out of place. The man made me feel like a sack of dirty laundry. It was a fair bet that his clothes and accessories cost more than I had in my bank account.

"Thank you for coming, Mr. Stone. This is out of character for me. I'm afraid I don't know where to begin. I've never spoken to a private investigator before. I've never had reason to speak to one."

"Don't worry, professor. Take your time. Most people I meet for the first time have never spoken to a private investigator. I'm like any other Joe on the street, just a guy trying to do a job."

He fidgeted and drummed his fingers on his desk. He glanced at me then broke eye contact and sat back and crossed his legs and folded his arms across his chest. He may have called me and asked me to come to his office, but now that I was sitting across from him he was reluctant to speak. He removed the watch from his vest pocket and glanced at it.

"That's a beautiful watch you're wearing," I said. "I own a modest collection of timepieces, but I've never seen a watch like yours."

He smiled.

"No, there aren't many like this one. Some people say only a handful exist. Others swear none exist at all, yet, here we are discussing the one I'm wearing. Are you familiar with the Wichita Watch Company?"

I raised an eyebrow and shook my head.

"Not many people are familiar with it. It has faded from memory. It existed for a very brief time some fifty years ago. A few city fathers and investors built a facility west of downtown, but before they could install manufacturing equipment, the economy turned sour. Many businesses struggled during that period, and a new business just opening its doors never stood a chance. The investors, bankers, cattle men, and land speculators, cut their losses to save their own businesses. The company went bust before it opened."

"If they never installed equipment, how did your watch come to be?" I said.

"Probably a prototype designed to attract investors. I bought mine years ago from one of those investors, a retired banker, who said he'd grown tired of looking at the damn thing. He hoped he'd never see it again. Who knows? Maybe it'll be worth something someday."

I nodded and said nothing.

"Well, look what you've done," he said. "You've got me talking."

"Start at the beginning," I said, "and take your time. Why did you call me? More importantly, what do you know about the woman's murder that the police don't know?"

He paused to gather his thoughts. I sat and waited.

"You said on the phone that you are familiar with the murder of Rosemary Joy. That was the young lady's name, by the way, Rosemary Joy Cleveland. You said you know about the murder?"

"I said I read the papers. Like I mentioned, the police arrested a suspect, and the evidence against him looks solid. That's the report. The case appears to be open and shut."

He nodded.

"Yes, yes," he said, "that's the report in the newspapers, alright, open and shut, except I don't believe that assessment is accurate. I believe the police have the wrong man in custody."

I listened to the fan hum and waited for him to continue. How and why had he reached that conclusion? He was an educated man. Did he know something, or was he batty? He seemed distraught but not off his rocker. If he hadn't wanted to divulge anything, he wouldn't have called me. Maybe he didn't know how to tell me what he knew. I figured he wouldn't lie to me, but he probably wouldn't tell me the whole truth, either. I'd have to be patient. The fan continued to hum.

"You probably think I'm crazy," he said.

I didn't reply.

"I knew her," he said. "Not well, but I knew her."

Fallon straightened the already neat stack of papers on his desk.

"Rosemary Joy was a student of mine, not this term. She graduated in the spring. That's how she preferred to be addressed, by the way, with both names, Rosemary Joy. She was such a lovely woman. You saw her picture in the paper?"

I nodded.

"Then you understand she was a part of a distinct minority here at the university. We have other Negro students, of course, but not many. Rosemary Joy was a nursing student. She enrolled in one of my advanced literature classes as an elective. I wondered why she enrolled in that class. It is intended for students majoring in English. She lacked the necessary prerequisites, so I called her into my office before our first session. What a pleasant surprise. I learned that she was well-read and knew the works of several contemporary American authors, Zora Neale Hurston and William Faulkner are two I recall. She had a burning desire to study other authors and their works. Her enthusiasm won me over, and I waived the requirements and allowed her to take the course. I didn't regret it. She was intelligent, inquisitive, and always prepared for class discussions, admirable qualities often lacking in the average student."

Fallon tented his fingers beneath his chin and stared at his desk.

"She didn't have much money. She worked as a caretaker for an elderly widow, earned room and board and a little extra for incidentals."

He raised his eyes to mine.

"During Rosemary Joy's senior year, the widow died, and that meager income went away. She found part-time work in another home, but her last year as a student was a struggle. She was no quitter. She stayed with it and graduated with honors."

Fallon smiled and seemed proud of his former student's determination.

"So, you knew her and admired her," I said. "That's nice. I would think you'd find satisfaction in knowing that the police have her killer in custody."

His eyes met mine.

"That's just it," he said. "I am not satisfied. I believe her killer is still out there somewhere. I believe the man in custody is innocent."

"Why do you think that?" I said. "Who do you think is the killer?"

"I don't know who the killer is. That's why I called you. I want you to find her murderer."

I felt like a drowning man treading water with no shore in sight.

"Tell me why you think the suspect is innocent," I said. "Tell me what you know about him. And if you tell me you don't know anything about him, I'm walking out of this office. You can find another gumshoe to toy with."

I had vowed to myself to be patient, but my patience had limits. Fallon recognized that and nodded.

"I've never met or spoken to the suspect," he said. "Rosemary Joy knew him. They were often together. His name is Henry Brown, by the way, although Rosemary Joy referred to him as Peanut. I don't know why she used that name, but she called him that with affection. When she was a student, I'd see him from time to time, always at a distance. He'd hang back and wait for her to come to him. It was as if he felt the university belonged to Rosemary Joy, and he wasn't a part of it, as if it were off-limits to him. It was her place to be, not his. She confirmed this when I asked about him. The university was her world, he'd told her, and he didn't belong. Sometimes in the afternoon, Rosemary Joy and I left the building at the same time. I'd watch Henry Brown pick her up after class, but I never saw him come near the building. He stood next to his car. When she approached, he'd take her books and give her a hug or a peck on the cheek. Then he'd open her door for her, always the gentleman."

"The papers mentioned that they knew each other," I said. "There's nothing unusual there. Murders are usually committed by someone known to the victim."

"I'm sure you're right," he said, "but that's just it. This wasn't that kind of relationship. I haven't made myself clear. The relationship between Mr. Brown and Miss Cleveland didn't seem to be based on sexual intimacy. On the few occasions when I saw them together, Brown seemed to be protective, Rosemary Joy's guardian, if you will. I sensed that if anyone ever tried to harm Rosemary Joy, they'd have to go through Henry Brown to do it. I can't believe that he'd harm the woman he seemed to care for."

I mulled that over.

"Based on what you observed, you may be correct," I said. "Brown may have been her protector, as you say. Still, one never knows how people behave in private. Tempers flare. Passion takes hold. Bad things happen. Your observations may be genuine, but I doubt they'd carry much weight with the police. Did you see the pair at any time off campus?"

"No, no. I only visited with Rosemary Joy in the classroom and in my office. Like I said, I've never spoken to Henry Brown."

He gazed at his desk and took a deep breath. The faint sounds of a marching band came through the window. Probably rehearsing for Saturday's football game, I thought. Fallon met my eyes.

"If you investigate this for me," he said, "I will pay whatever fee you ask. If you remain convinced that Brown is guilty, I will accept your decision. I give you my word I will not pursue the matter further. In the name of justice, I have to know with absolute certainty that the man the police have arrested is Rosemary Joy Cleveland's murderer."

We were interrupted by a knock at the door. Fallon rose and opened the door slightly. A glance at my watch told me it was twelve-forty. A voice came from the hallway, a male voice speaking in a deferential tone.

"I graded those quizzes, Dr. Fallon, and I put them in your box. I have a class at one o'clock. Will you need anything else today?"

"No, no, thank you, Arthur. That's all for today. I'll see you tomorrow. Bring your research to me along with your draft and notes. We'll discuss your progress. Come to my office before ten o'clock in the morning."

"Yes, sir. Will do, professor."

Fallon closed the door and returned to his chair.

"Well?" he said.

"Frankly, professor, I think you're wasting your money, and I suspect there's more you're not telling me. Also, I planned on taking some time off this week."

He said nothing.

"I'll spend a day or so asking questions," I said. "See what I can find out. I'll check around, but I'd advise you to be prepared for disappointment."

I told Fallon I'd report back to him in a couple of days, but he insisted on giving me a week's retainer and wrote the check without hesitation. I intended to take no more than a day or two to ask some questions and get some answers, even if they weren't the answers that Fallon wanted to hear. There was no doubt in my mind that the murderer was downtown behind bars.

We concluded our business and shook hands. I left his office and took the stairs back to the first floor. Ethan Alexander's door was ajar, so I knocked and stuck my head through the doorway. His office was empty. That was unfortunate. I'd hoped to ask him a few questions about his colleague, but I didn't intend to cool my heels while Alexander delivered a history lecture. I placed a business card on his desk and left the building.

I got into my car and rolled away when I noticed Professor Fallon exiting the building. I slowed and turned to watch him. He had his arm wrapped around the copy of Untermeyer's poetry anthology. He strolled toward the tan Hudson I'd noticed earlier, probably headed for lunch. I continued driving.

Misguided though he was, the professor seemed sincere. He believed Henry Brown was innocent, and I admired his conviction. He was determined to find the truth for himself. It shouldn't take long to investigate the matter, I mused. The cops had the right man behind bars. I drove past the football field where the marching band rehearsed for Saturday's big game and rolled off campus beneath a banner exhorting the Wichita Shockers to crush the Kansas Jayhawks. With luck, I would wrap up the case before the first pitch of the World Series on Wednesday, two days away. Little did I know how mistaken I was.

You Know Perfectly Well

T he local news had reported the murder, of course, and I'd read the stories just as I explained to the professor, but after the police assured the public that the sole suspect was behind bars, I hadn't given the reports more thought. News of a murder, although tragic, is soon replaced by more urgent, personal thoughts like I need a haircut and don't forget to buy a can of coffee. Quotidian and mundane needs moved to the fore, and my thoughts turned elsewhere. I needed to reread the reports and make some calls before I wasted any shoe leather.

The man Wilfred Fallon was a mystery that called for investigation. Even though he had hired me, I had no intention of being played by a man I didn't know.

The dance in my stomach reminded me that I hadn't eaten since the previous afternoon, but I had another stop to make before lunch. I pulled up in front of Doc's Clocks near the university. Many of my clocks came from Doc's shop, most purchased from his stock on hand. That day, however, I was on a search for a specific clock for a special someone. I opened the door, and a cuckoo's chirp alerted the owner of my presence. A rustling sound came from the backroom, and Doc shuffled in through a doorway behind the counter, a slight, hunched man. Wisps of gray hair decorated his spotted skull, and a jeweler's loupe dangled from the chain around his neck. He retrieved wire-rimmed glasses from his apron and fitted the temple tips behind his ears.

"Pete Stone, hello, hello! Good to see you. It's been too long."

He extended his hand, and I shook it.

"Hello, Doc. It's good to see you, too. I hope you've been well. How are you?"

His eyes twinkled.

"Who knows? Only time will tell," he said.

I groaned at his pun. We chatted a moment, and I told him why I had stopped by.

"I'm looking for a specific clock, Doc, a piece to fit on a mantel. I need a Chelsea Brass Marine mounted on a mahogany base. It's to be a gift. Do you think you could locate one for me?"

He scratched his cheek and gazed down to the side.

"Chelsea Brass Marine, Chelsea Brass Marine, hmm. If memory serves, you've asked about that clock before. Weren't you looking for one some time ago?" he said.

"You have a good memory, Doc. Yes, I did ask about it. At the time I was considering it for myself, but now I need one for a friend."

"Well, it's a nice timepiece, and it will make a handsome gift," he said, then he grinned. "Why do I suspect this gift is for a woman?"

I said nothing, and he laughed.

"Never mind, never mind," he said. "That's none of my business. A Chelsea Brass Marine isn't rare, but I don't have one on hand. It may take a day or two to locate one. I'll look for the clock, and if it isn't mounted the way you want, I'll mount it for you in my shop. Let me see what I can find, and I'll give you a call."

I shook his hand.

"Swell, Doc. Thanks," I said.

We chatted for another moment, and I left. The dancing jig in my stomach gave way to a crooner singing the blues, so I headed downtown for a bite to eat. Midafternoon traffic moved along, but by the time I pulled up to the curb on Douglas, I was fatigued by lack of nourishment and too little sleep. I parked in front of the Hotel Eaton and down the block from my office on the corner at Emporia. It was long past the noon rush.

A couple of businessmen in suits huddled over cups of coffee and paper-clipped pages on the table between them, a contract, perhaps. A middle-aged woman in a green dress and matching hat sat at a table in the corner next to a window and sipped a cup of tea, her movements slow and deliberate. She placed her cup on its saucer with an easy elegance and gazed out at the downtown scene and twisted the gold band on her ring finger.

A waitress seated me and took my order for a bowl of chili and a cup of coffee. I lit a cigarette and read over my notes. Professor Fallon's passion for uncovering the truth was commendable, but I didn't for a minute believe that he'd told me everything he knew. He had an admiration for his former student, Rosemary Joy Cleveland, as did many a teacher for a talented and dedicated student. Nothing unusual there. That didn't explain his determination to prove the innocence of Henry Brown, a man who Fallon said he'd never met, only observed from a distance.

My lunch arrived, and I ate it quickly. The chili was delicious, but my thoughts weren't on food. I mulled over my next move. After checking in at the office and making some calls, I would visit the scene of the crime. After that, I'd see about visiting Henry Brown in jail. I finished the chili and smoked another cigarette with my coffee. The meal gave me a needed boost, and I started to feel human again.

The lady in the green dress finished her tea and leaned back in her chair. She folded her napkin and placed it next to her cup and saucer and rose from her chair. She passed by my table, and a

27

quick glance revealed a pale circle on her finger where the ring had rested before. *C'est la vie, c'est l'amour*, I mused. I finished my coffee. The men in suits were still discussing their contract when I paid my bill.

I left the hotel and walked to the other end of the block. My office was on the third floor of the Lawrence Block Building situated on the corner. I entered and started for the elevator when I recalled the university coed who held the door for me that morning. I nodded at the elevator operator and walked past him to the stairs. Two floors later I still had pep in my step, not bad for a guy my age, I thought. I opened the door beneath the sign that read, "Pete Stone, Private Investigations." Take that, I whispered to the coed in my mind. Agnes, my secretary, sat at her desk in the outer office thumbing through a bridal catalog.

"Hello, Pete," she said. "Goodness, why are you so out of breath? Sit down. Should I get you a glass of water?"

I shook my head, and my shoulders slumped. So much for the pep in my step, I thought. Maybe I was getting old. I returned her hello and ignored the offer of water.

"A man stopped by earlier and dropped this off," she said and handed me an envelope. It was unaddressed but bore the logo of the warehouse that had had its truck stolen. I opened it and counted the money. It looked right. I handed the envelope back to Agnes and told her to put it in the safe.

"What's with the dresses and veils?" I said and nodded toward the catalog. "Somebody getting married?"

Agnes closed the catalog and tossed it aside.

"Pete Stone, don't start with me. You know perfectly well I'm getting married, and you know to whom. Furthermore, dear boss, I've already been fitted for a gown. I was just browsing. I hope you haven't forgotten that you're giving me away at the wedding."

"Oh, right, I do recall you mentioning something about getting married. To a banker, I believe. Percy something, wasn't it?"

Agnes rose from behind her desk and stood with her face close to mine.

"His name, as you well know, is Percival Gillman. He is my fiancé, my betrothed, soon to be my husband. On my wedding day, three weeks from yesterday in case you've forgotten, you will walk me arm-in-arm down the aisle and give me away."

Our noses were inches apart.

"Remind me again. How am I supposed to give someone away who's never belonged to me in the first place?" I said.

Agnes gave me a tender slap.

"You know better than that," she said. "I could have belonged to you. All you had to do was ask."

"Huh? Are you sure about that? All I had to do was ask? What would you have said?"

I gave her a grin, but she looked serious.

"There was a time when the answer would have been yes," Agnes said.

"I'm a sap," I said. "I should have asked. All my life I've never known what I wanted. It turns out that's exactly what I got."

"You're a sap, alright, but you can't turn back the clock. You know that. We both know there is another woman in your future, even if she doesn't know it yet. I'm betting that someday soon, she'll come around. She's the one for you, Pete. You know it, and I know it."

We gave each other a quick hug and stepped apart.

"You are a wise woman," I said. "How come women are so much smarter than men?"

"God gave men the brawn. We got the brains."

"You'll get no argument from me."

We went back to business. Agnes returned to her desk, and I went into my inner office.

"Bring me the recent issues of *The Eagle*," I said over my shoulder. "The ones covering the murder of that university coed, please."

"Right away."

I took a seat behind my desk and noticed I was perspiring. I wiped my forehead with my handkerchief. Agnes came in with several newspapers and placed them on my desk.

"Are you sure you're okay?" she said. "How about that glass of water?"

"No, I'm fine," I said, "thanks, kiddo."

She frowned down at me.

"I'm worried about you. You need to take care of yourself. You're not a young man anymore."

"So I've been reminded. Really, I'm fine."

The outer door opened, and she left me and closed my door behind her. I heard a boy's voice and glanced out the window to the sidewalk below. A familiar green bike leaned against a lamp-post. Rusty was delivering the afternoon edition of the newspaper.

The newspapers on my desk were stacked in order with the most recent edition on top. I had read them earlier, so I thumbed through them quickly. Sunday's paper had an advertisement for a movie at the Miller Theater that I recalled looked interesting, *Souls at Sea*, with Gary Cooper, George Raft, and Frances Dee. The 1938 Studebaker models had arrived at Friendly motors on East Douglas, and there was another oil strike in Barton County. The Kansas Authors Club had held their annual convention that weekend, and officers of the club were pictured in their finery. The club had gone on record as favoring a Secretary of Peace to take place alongside other secretaries in Franklin Roosevelt's cabinet. Good for them, I thought. I skipped over the sports pages and was reminded by another article that railroad workers had negotiated a twenty percent raise. Wages would go up forty-four cents a day.

I continued skimming the newspapers until I came to the copy with the story about the murder. Page seven. A stabbing always got print, but the stabbing of one Negro by another Negro didn't make the front page. That news probably went unnoticed in parts of town, but I read the newspaper from front to back. It took only a few minutes to reread the report and make some notes in my book. I thumbed another paper for the follow up, the capture of the suspect on page eleven. The report slipped deeper into the paper.

When I finished with the newspapers, I picked up the phone and dialed a number and asked for Marjorie. A couple of moments later, a feminine voice came on the line.

"Marjorie speaking."

"Hello, Marjorie. Pete Stone calling on behalf of Abe Lincoln."

Her voice lowered.

"Uh-huh. And what should a girl do to warrant a visit from Mr. Lincoln?"

"I'm looking for anything you might have on Wilfred Fallon, a professor at the city university. My guess is you'll come up empty, but even that would tell me something. I'm in my office."

"Give me a few minutes," she said.

I hung up the phone. Marjorie Mattox worked at the city police station and occasionally enjoyed coffee and cake with her dear friend, Lois Newkirk, who also happened to be my landlady. I met Marjorie in Lois's kitchen one day when I stopped by to pay the rent and learned that she was a widow who supported herself as a file clerk. She was an elderly woman with porcelain skin, blue veins, and hair to match. She asked what I did for a living, and when I told her I was a private detective, she told me she worked at the police station. Nothing else was mentioned at the time, but our smiles suggested we had come to a mutual understanding. I never leaned on Marjorie for information I couldn't get through other channels, but hers came quickly, with efficiency and discretion. I relied on her silence, and she appreciated the few extra bucks.

I lit a cigarette, and the telephone rang before I finished it. I picked it up on the first ring and heard Agnes return her receiver to its cradle.

"Marjorie?"

"Yes, Pete. I looked up the name you gave me, and I came up empty, just as you suspected. We have no file on your man."

"That's fine. Like I said, that tells me something. Thanks. I'll stop by soon."

"I know you will. Till then."

I hung up the phone and grabbed my hat. A glance out the window told me that the shadows had grown longer, but the day wasn't over. Agnes was on the phone. She told her party at the other end of the line that it would be a small church wedding, then said she had to go and hung up the phone.

"Sorry," she said. "That was my sister. Details, details."

"No worries, kid. I'm off to do some sleuthing. Lock up when you're finished, and I'll see you tomorrow."

I reached for the doorknob, and she spoke my name and paused.

"Pete."

I turned back.

"Don't work too late," she said. "You need sleep. Go home. Go to bed. You've been working all day, and I know you only had a couple of hours of sleep last night. You can't keep going without getting some rest."

"Mother, dear, are you treating me like a child?"

"Just the opposite," she said. "I'm telling you that you are no longer a child. It's time you started acting like a grown-up."

Her look was too serious, so I grinned at her. It didn't work. She returned a frown.

"Duly noted," I said. "Is that all?"

"No. Get a haircut, and get a shoeshine."

I glanced at my shoes.

"Yes, mother," I said and blew her a kiss as I went out the door.

I passed by the elevator and took the stairs. Walking down the stairs was a snap. Gravity is kinder going down than it is on the way up. Out on the street, I caught my reflection in a store window. I stopped and took off my hat and looked at my image. Agnes was right. I did need a haircut. I looked at my shoes again. They were scuffed. Agnes was always right.

You May Call Me Miss Edna

I headed east on Douglas and dropped south on Washington. Shadows lengthened and brought cooler air, so I'd put the top up on the roadster and snapped it into place before I left downtown. I turned left off Washington and worked my way a few blocks further to a residential neighborhood on Lulu Street. The address of a large dwelling on a corner matched the address given in the newspapers, so I pulled over to the curb and shut off the engine.

The imposing structure seemed out of place in the neighborhood. Frame homes, mostly white or pastel in color, stretched up and down the streets in four directions. Each appeared to be a single-family home. The house on the corner loomed larger than others nearby and was constructed of dark stone rather than wood. Archways surrounded the front porch on three sides, and from above, circular windows looked out on the street. A hand-painted sign in front read, "Room and Board. Ladies only."

School had let out for the day, and children played nearby. It was a mixed neighborhood, and Negro kids played with white kids. That was the thing about children. They hadn't learned that they weren't supposed to like each other. A couple of youngsters tossed an old baseball. Its long gone horsehide had been replaced with dark tape. The tape had started to unravel. A trio of girls played hopscotch on the sidewalk, and a boy in the street rolled a hoop with a stick.

I went up the sidewalk and climbed the steps beneath the center archway and knocked on the door. A dog barked from within the house. The door opened a foot or so, and a brown face framed with white curls peeked out at me. The snout of a large dog appeared beneath the face. The dog barked again, but the woman told it to hush. It did and backed away.

"Yes?" the woman said. "What do you want?"

"Hello, ma'am," I said. "My name is Pete Stone. I'm investigating the recent tragedy. I need to ask you a few questions regarding the recent death of your boarder."

"Recent death? You mean murder, don't you?" she said.

"Yes, that's right, her murder."

She looked me up and down and seemed to disapprove of what she saw.

"You a cop? You look like a cop. I've already spoken to a cop and answered his questions, most of 'em more than once."

"Yes, I'm sure you have," I said, "but I need to ask some more questions."

"Why?"

"I'm a private investigator. My questions will only take a few minutes. I won't take much of your time."

"Hmm- mmm. You're right about that," she said and started to close the door.

"Wait," I said and placed my hand on the door. I met surprising resistance. She was a lightweight, but she was tough and wiry. She looked at my hand and back at me. She did not appear pleased.

"Listen, mister. I've got a dog in here. A big dog."

"Yes, I know you do," I said, "and if you gave the command, that big dog of yours would probably lick me to death. Look, I'm not here to upset you. I just need a few minutes to ask some questions on behalf of my client. After that you'll never see me again."

"I couldn't be that lucky. What kind of investigator are you anyway? Don't you know them cops already got that killer locked up in their jailhouse? Why don't you go on and talk to them? What you want to be pestering an old woman for?"

"I know the police have their suspect in jail, but my client believes the police have made a mistake. He thinks that their suspect is innocent. I'm just looking for the truth. If my client is correct, you'd help prevent an innocent man from being wrongly convicted."

She let out a harsh laugh and pulled open the door and stood with her fists on her hips.

"Mister, you must be plumb loco. You must be out of your mind if you think those police are ever going to release that young man. That ain't gonna happen. Not today, not ever. He might as well be strapped in that 'lectric chair right now. They gonna fry that boy."

I said nothing. I waited. She shook her head and stepped back to let me enter.

"I must be a fool for gabbing with a crazy man. Come on in, Mr. Crazy Man, and pester an old fool with your questions."

I crossed the threshold and took off my hat. She was a small woman, with limbs like barbed wire and a face like a sack of prunes. I introduced myself and gave her my card. She snatched it with a bony claw, gave it a cursory glance, and slipped it into a pocket of her housedress. I took in the room. To the right, several frayed, overstuffed chairs were arrayed around an unlit fireplace. A Philco console radio stood against the wall. The dog, a black Labrador with a graying muzzle, dozed on a rug in front of the fireplace, remarkably at peace for a would-be guard dog and protector of the castle. A sofa rested against the front wall beneath a picture window. A table with four straight-backed chairs sat along the wall to the left. A partially completed jigsaw puzzle lay on the table. Straight ahead, a hallway led to the rear of the house. Stairs midway down the hall rose to the upper floor. A handwritten notice on the wall next to the hallway cautioned gentlemen guests to remain in the parlor.

Cooking smells wafted from down the hall along with sounds of female voices and laughter and the clangs of pots and pans. The woman lowered herself into one of the stuffed chairs and flicked her wrist toward another one. I sat down.

"The clock's ticking," she said. "I got supper on the stove and girls to feed."

I'd have bet my last dollar that this woman hadn't cooked a meal for herself or her boarders in years. Room and board likely meant clean your room, cook the meals, and wash the dishes after.

"You haven't given me your name," I said. "How shall I address you?"

"You may call me Miss Edna."

"Thank you, Miss Edna. First, let me say that I'm sorry about the recent tragedy. What happened was awful. I'm sure you've been under a strain, but I need to gather information. I'd like to know something about the deceased. What can you tell me about Rosemary Joy?"

The old woman met my eyes. The sack of prunes relaxed a bit and cracked into what might have been a smile.

"How'd you know to call her Rosemary Joy? Not everybody knew to call her Rosemary Joy, not at first, they didn't. People who didn't know better called her Rosemary, but she always corrected them. Yes, sir. That's the first thing I can tell you about her. If you called that girl by name, you called her Rosemary Joy. She mentioned once that her mother's name was Joy, rest her soul, and she intended to hear her mother's name spoken every day. She always used both of her given names and expected others to do the same."

"She must have loved her mother. What else? What do you know about her family?"

"Didn't have any as far as I know. She was quiet, kept to herself. Didn't talk about herself much. She mentioned that her parents had died, that's all. Never said how or why, just that they were dead."

"Did she talk about other family members?"

"No, not to me. Not to the other ladies either, and that's what they told the police. Police asked about family, too, you know, but we couldn't tell them anything."

"How long did you know Rosemary Joy? How long was she your boarder?"

"Just a short time, not even a month. She lived with an older couple before that, on account of her work."

"What work was that?" I said.

"She worked as a nurse, a private duty nurse, for the elderly or sick folks, folks near death, you know, cancer and such. She lived in their homes and cared for them 'round the clock. Must have been lonely work. Sad, too, I suppose. It seemed to suit Rosemary Joy, though. She was a serious woman, old for her age. Didn't laugh much. Her last job was looking after an old woman who lived with her daughter, daytime care only. The daughter worked during the day but was home nights. So Rosemary Joy came to me for a room."

"How about friends, other boarders? Were any of the women close to Rosemary Joy? A friend or confidant?"

Miss Edna arched her back.

"Not that I know of," she said, "and I'm not going to have you bothering my girls with your questions, either. They all spoke to the policeman, and they all said the same thing. They didn't see or hear a thing. They were all asleep in their beds at the time of the murder."

She adopted the pose of a mother hen protecting her chicks. I took another tack.

"What do you know about the suspect, Henry Brown? The papers said Brown and Rosemary Joy knew each other."

She nodded.

"Yes, that's right. They knew each other," she said. She looked down at the floor and shook her white head. "Mmm, mmm, mmm. What a puzzlement. What would make that man do such a horrible thing to that young woman? Mmm, mmm, mmm."

"What can you tell me about him?"

She stared at the floor a moment longer, then looked back at me.

"He came around to check on Rosemary Joy, see if she was alright, and did she need anything, you know. He seemed to protect her, that's how it seemed to me. That's why this is all so crazy to believe. They seemed friendly to each other, more than friendly, affectionate. Friends, you see, but not like they was a he and a she couple. They'd hug, maybe a peck on the cheek or a squeeze of the hand, that's all."

She shook her head again.

"You never can tell. She called him Peanut, I believe I heard. That's right, Peanut. I couldn't tell you why. He was thoughtful. Telephoned before stopping by unless Rosemary Joy called him first. Never stopped by unannounced. He was quiet, too, and shy. Never spoke to anyone else except a polite hello."

"It sounds like they cared for one another. Maybe my client is right. Maybe Brown didn't kill her," I said.

Miss Edna raised her eyebrows, and her mouth fell open.

"What kind of crazy talk is that? Of course, he stabbed that woman! He had the knife right in his hand! He stood right over her with the knife in his hand!"

"You saw this?"

The papers hadn't divulged that detail, only that the body was discovered by the owner of the boardinghouse, and the police arrested Brown after he was seen fleeing the premises.

"Yes, I discovered the body," she said, "and I saw that man holding the knife. Ruff there," she nodded toward the dog, "he barked and woke me up. Ruff sleeps in my room, right at the foot of my bed. I sat up in bed when I heard his barking and listened. I heard noises in the house, so I got up to check. Rosemary Joy's door was open, and her light was on, so I looked in, and there he was, standing over her, holding that bloody knife."

Her eyes grew big and stared at nothing.

"What happened then?"

Her gaze came back to me.

"I screamed, that's what happened. I thought I was a goner. I surely did. That boy dropped the knife and ran. Ran right past me."

"He didn't harm you?"

"No, he just pushed me aside, brushed me out of the way and ran. Went out the back door. Ruff barked, but that's all he did." She grinned and shook her head. "You're right about Ruff, you know. He's harmless, that dog is. He'd sooner dance the Tennessee Waltz than take a bite out of a person."

"When did this take place, what time of day?"

"Early morning, not long before the house came awake. My scream woke one or two of my ladies. Not long after that alarm clocks started ringing."

Miss Edna glanced at a clock on the wall. She pushed herself from the chair and rose to her feet.

"Speaking of time, ours is up. I've got to feed my ladies."

"Just one last thing," I said. "I'd like to look at Rosemary Joy's room. It'll only take a minute."

"There's nothing to see. The police sealed that room off," she said. "Took everything but the furniture. Took all of that girl's personals. Just as well. I'll probably never rent that room again."

"The police have completed their investigation," I said. "The room is empty. I'll only be a moment."

She heaved an elaborate sigh and turned toward the hallway. She shook her head and mumbled something.

"Come on then," she said. "Make it fast. Supper's waitin'."

I followed her down the hall and was surprised when she didn't take the stairs to the upper floor. I'd assumed the bedrooms were upstairs and we'd go to the second floor. We continued down the hall past a bathroom and laundry room on the left and the kitchen and dining area on the right. Two women were placing dinnerware on a long table surrounded by eight chairs. At the end of the hall was the back door. A window to the left of the door looked out on an alley. To the right of the back entrance, another doorway led to a room at the back corner of the house. Miss Edna entered that room, and I followed.

"This is it," she said.

In earlier days, the room had probably served as a pantry or for storage, but it had been converted to a small bedroom. It held a single bed with a bare mattress along the wall opposite the door and a table with a pair of chairs to the left. An open door to the right revealed a closet. A small dresser stood against the wall next to the closet door. The room had two windows, one over the bed and one over the table to the left. The bare wood floor looked freshly scrubbed. A light fixture and fan hung in the center of the ceiling.

"Is this how the room looked before the police took it apart?" I asked.

Miss Edna nodded.

"Mostly. There was a small rug right here where her body was."

She indicated a spot in the center of the floor beneath the light and fan.

"And then there was her personals, of course, not much. A couple of dresses and her underthings, cosmetics, and such. The police took all that."

"Nothing else?" I said.

Miss Edna shook her head. I thought for a moment. Something else was missing.

"How about books," I said, "or magazines, maybe a Bible?"

The old woman shook her head. "She did read a small Bible. I suppose they took that, too. I never noticed any other reading material."

She looked thoughtful.

"Had you seen Rosemary Joy reading on earlier occasions?"

"Yes, I suppose I did, now that you mention it. She did enjoy reading, like you say, a book or her Bible. I suppose her books came from the library."

I opened and shut each of the drawers in the dresser, expecting to find nothing and was unsurprised when I didn't. The drawers were empty.

"How about writing materials? Stationery or a diary?"

"She may have had those things, but I don't recall them."

That seemed odd. I looked around the room again.

"Why did Rosemary Joy live here in this room? Aren't the bedrooms upstairs?"

"Yes, they are, and so is mine. The house was full up when she came to me. That's why she had this room. It was the only one I had available."

I looked at the window opposite the doorway. I stepped over to the bed and pulled it away from the wall so I could I search the window for indications of forced entry. I found none and pushed the bed back to its original position. I checked the other window and found nothing unusual there either. I walked into the hallway and opened the backdoor and looked up and down the alley. An inspection of the lock on the door revealed several scratches.

"The police said he came in through this door," Miss Edna said from behind me.

I nodded agreement. I closed the door, and we went back down the hallway toward the parlor. Another woman had joined the pair in the dining room. The table was set for four. I wanted to question each of them, but Miss Edna, slight as she was, looked like she'd toss me out on my ear if I tried. We continued to the parlor, and I plucked my hat from the chair.

"Thank you for your time, Miss Edna," I said and put on my hat. "You've been most helpful."

"Uh-huh," she said. "And you've been a nuisance and made me late for my supper. You better hope my food isn't cold or there'll soon be more violence committed in this house."

She yanked open the door with one hand and struck a pose with her other hand on her hip. I hustled past her and made it to the porch before the swinging door caught my backside. At the top of the steps, I paused and lit a cigarette and gazed down the street. Afternoon shadows had given way to twilight. Homes were lighted, and the children I had seen earlier had gone indoors.

I walked down the steps and got in the roadster and pondered questions as I drove. Miss Edna's impressions of Rosemary Joy and Henry Brown and their relationship mirrored those of Professor Fallon. A young couple, mutual affection. Most victims knew their murderers, but there seemed to be a genuine tenderness there. Rosemary Joy called him Peanut.

The old woman came upon the scene early in the morning, only a few minutes before everyone woke up to start their day. That seemed an odd time to commit murder, at least a premeditated murder. A crime committed a few hours earlier in the night, before the house came awake, had a better chance of going undetected than a crime committed moments before alarm clocks sounded. The murder must have been a spontaneous act, a crime of passion. If it was spontaneous, that didn't explain why Brown was in the boardinghouse at that hour. Miss Edna said he never came to the house unannounced.

The lack of reading and writing material puzzled me. Rosemary Joy owned few possessions. I could understand that. A young working woman might not have much, but this woman would have had something to read. No reading material in the room didn't jibe with Professor Fallon's account of his star student. According to the professor, Rosemary Joy loved literature. A person who loved to read always managed to have a book or a magazine available. She'd sooner skip a meal than be without reading material. No writing materials, either. That didn't add up.

The table in the dining room allowed seating for eight people. That night the table was set for four, presumably three boarders and Miss Edna. Where were the other boarders? Was the house no longer full? Miss Edna said the house was full when Rosemary Joy lived there. That's why she roomed downstairs. Boardinghouses experience lots of turnover, and a recent murder may have spooked the residents. Which boarders left, and where had they gone?

None of my questions pointed to the innocence of Henry Brown, but they nagged at me. They wanted answers.

The Sphinx is Not in Cairo

I t turned out I had been wrong. A good night's sleep was not as overrated as I had thought. It was exactly what I needed. Following my visit with Miss Edna, I'd planned on stopping in at Tom's Inn for a cold beer and a bite to eat, but after I left the boardinghouse, my roadster steered itself to my place where I collapsed into bed and fell into a deep, dreamless sleep. Ten hours later I awoke to the soft chimes of my clocks and rose from bed feeling human again.

My stakeout on Sunday evening and into Monday morning had taken a toll. It seemed not long ago that losing a night's sleep had little effect on me. All I needed was an hour or two in the sack, and I'd answer the bell and come out swinging. Whether those days were recently or a lifetime ago, the point was moot. The face in the mirror wasn't growing younger. From here on in, I'd leave it to Alley Oop in the funny pages to carry the stone hammer and fight the dinosaurs. The rules were changing for me. It had become a younger man's game.

I showered and shaved and dressed. Then I telephoned Agnes at the office and told her I had some places to go first, but I'd see her later. I followed the telephone call with three cups of black coffee, a couple of scrambled eggs with toast and a cigarette. By the time I opened the door to face the day, I felt rested, fresh, and mildly invincible. The wrinkled face that had clouded my mirror was barely a memory. I took in a lungful of crisp air and clicked my heels and toes on the stairs with pep in my step. I hopped into my car and kept my eyes peeled for dragons as I drove.

The roadster was eighteen years old, had some miles on it, and showed some wear, but so did a comfortable pair of shoes. The previous owner had kept it well-maintained, and I did the same. A couple of years ago, I'd done some work, several weeks work, for the man who once owned the car. The guy also owned a Bentley, a Cadillac, and a ranch that could have been the younger brother to Rhode Island. He'd hired me to recover stolen jewelry. The job took time and a trip to the west coast, but he was grateful when I returned with the gems. He had wealth and plenty of it, but at that moment, he was short on cash, another victim of the market crash and the Depression. In lieu of cash, he offered me the keys to the Jones Sports Roadster as payment for my services. The car was worth more than my fee, but who was I to argue? It took me less time than a mayfly on a date to agree and say yes.

The Jones Motor Car Company made its first automobile in Wichita in 1914. Their cars were well-built and sold well, but six years after opening its doors a fire destroyed most of the business, and it never recovered. Once I acquired the roadster, I snooped around and found a former Jones Company mechanic who had a cache of parts and his own garage. He kept my machine tuned.

I dropped south on Waco a dozen blocks to Douglas and admired the city, what the founder of *The Wichita Eagle* had once dubbed, The Peerless Princess of the Plains. Marshall Murdock was no stranger to hyperbole, but the city did have a charm and a history of business entrepreneurship, along with tales of fortunes made and lost. Across the Arkansas River to the west, Lawrence Stadium loomed like a mausoleum, empty now, its season over. The only organized baseball remaining to be played was the World Series in New York City. The Yankees and the Giants would square off in the best-of-seven match due to begin the following day.

I drove east and parked on the street in front of the Hotel Eaton at Douglas and St. Francis. I got out of my car and headed for the hotel and crossed paths with a seedy looking character on the sidewalk. He caught my eye and touched the brim of his hat.

"Hey, pal, can you spare a dime?" he said.

I looked him over. The cuffs on his jacket and the collar on his shirt were frayed, and his hat was stained with sweat. Five would get you ten his shoes had holes in their soles. Still, his eyes were clear, and he didn't reek of liquor. He was just one of thousands like him down on his luck.

"Had a meal lately?" I said.

He flicked the tip of his tongue over his lower lip.

"Depends on what you mean by lately, I guess."

I fished a dollar bill out of my wallet and jutted my chin toward a beanery across the street.

"They serve a decent meal over there at a fair price. I eat there myself from time to time."

He took the bill and nodded his thanks. I watched him cross the street. Sometimes I ignore a bum's plea for help. Sometimes I don't. I couldn't tell you why that is. He headed for the door of the restaurant but paused before he entered. He stooped to speak to a guy sitting on the sidewalk, another down-at-the-heels character. The guy on the walk nodded and rose to his feet, and the pair went into the beanery together. I'd given the panhandler a buck, a lousy dollar, and he was compelled to share his largesse with a stranger. I shook my head. What a world.

Inside the hotel, the spacious lobby held a few guests reading newspapers, chatting, or smoking. A gentleman read last month's issue of *The Atlantic Monthly*, an article written by Herbert Hoover. I'd read the piece. It called for Republicans to rally the party against the principles of Roosevelt's New Deal.

Ceiling fans hummed and kept the air circulating. A half-dozen leather couches and twice that many matching chairs were arrayed on the ornate tile floor or atop one of several Persian carpets. Large pillars throughout the lobby lent an air of elegance and intimacy to the decor.

I walked past the lobby desk and caught the eye of the manager. He nodded in my direction, and I raised two fingers to the brim of my hat. I crossed the lobby and went down a hallway beyond until I reached the door next to the striped pole on the wall. The barber was the only soul in the shop. He sat in the customer's chair and read a newspaper. I caught a headline, "Is America Headed for One Man Government?" He folded the newspaper and stood and greeted me when I came through the door. He swiped the already clean chair with a towel, and I took a seat.

A half an hour later, we'd hashed out the odds on who'd win the Series, solved the country's economic problems and mildly disagreed on the silver screen's top leading lady. The barber was a fan of Carole Lombard while I preferred Claudette Colbert, but we agreed that the country had lost a gem with the passing of Jean Harlow earlier that year. I left the shop with my ears lowered, my shoulders brushed, and sporting the aroma of bay rum.

A shoeshine stand was across the hall from the barber. Its proprietor grinned when I approached.

"I watched you go into the barbershop earlier, and I said to myself, that gentleman is spiffing up his appearance. He'll be wanting a shoeshine before long. He'll be here soon."

"If you saw me go into the barbershop, you also noticed the condition of my shoes, and you saw they needed more attention than my hair did."

He laughed at that.

"How are you, Waldo?" I said and stuck out my hand. He shook it.

"Right as rain and no use to complain. And yourself, Mr. Stone?"

"Getting along. How's our boy? Is he working?"

Ellis Waldo worked polish into the cracks and creases of my shoes with deft fingertips and pondered my question about Ralph Waldo, Ellis's son.

"He's working," he said, "but he's ambitious. He's always hungry for more."

"Good. If he's available, ask him to stop by my office later today, would you? I have a job that's tailor-made for a man of his talents."

Waldo nodded and gave me a wink. It was a pleasure to watch an expert at his craft, and Waldo took pride in his work. He made his shine rag sing, blurring it back and forth like a fiddler working a bow. The rag popped and snapped, and before long my shoes boasted a high gloss. When he finished, we both admired his work, and I complimented his effort.

"Now you're looking dapper from head to toe," he said, "like a million bucks." I agreed. I thanked him and paid him, and we shook hands again before I left.

I glanced at my image as I passed by a mirror in the lobby. Agnes knew what she was talking about. There was nothing like a shine and a haircut to make a man presentable, to boost his confidence and make him eager to face the world. Back outside, a young woman strolled down the sidewalk. I flashed my pearly whites and tipped my hat. The young lady huffed and gave me a harsh glance and turned her head as she walked by. I shrugged and climbed into the roadster.

It was only a half-dozen blocks from the hotel to the police station at William and Main. Under Franklin Roosevelt's New Deal program, the police station had undergone a renovation, and Wichita's finest were housed in a newly remodeled Art Deco structure adjacent to City Hall. I parked across the street from a row of police cars standing at the ready alongside the station.

The building had been renovated, but the air inside was stale and smelled like no one had cracked a window since the Roosevelt inauguration. Not Franklin's—Theodore's. Scents of stale coffee and cigarettes mingled with odors of the unwashed visitors from the city's streets. I stopped in front of the desk sergeant and asked if Mac was in, and he answered with a flip of a thumb over his shoulder. On the way to Mac's office, I nodded at familiar faces and paused at the desk of a woman with blue hair who was alphabetizing files.

"Hello, Marjorie. How have you been?" I said.

Marjorie Mattox looked up and smiled.

"Fine, Pete, and you?"

I stuck out my hand, and she shook it and made the five-dollar bill in my palm disappear. My job was easier with a discrete ally downtown. Even though she'd found nothing on Professor Fallon, I appreciated her efforts and paused to show my gratitude.

"Always a pleasure to see you," she said.

I continued to Mac's office. The frosted glass on the closed door read, Detective Lieutenant Thaddeus McCormick. I knocked on the glass and reached for the knob. A gruff voice from inside barked, "Yeah?"

I went in. Mac sat hunched over his desk and studied five or six black-and-white glossy photographs he held in knuckled fists, pictures taken by a crime scene photographer it appeared. He was a lanky package of bones, elbows, and knobbed knees splayed akimbo beneath a large head. Wisps of fine hair fought to gain purchase atop his broad skull. Smoke from the cigar in his mouth rose toward the ceiling.

"Mac, you're something. Most guys go gray when they age, but not you. You're going pink," I said.

He lifted his gaze from the photographs to me and offered a look like he'd bitten into an apple and discovered half a worm. He took the cigar out of his mouth.

"Just what I need to make this day perfect—a visit from a bumbling shamus, or is that redundant—bumbling shamus? Whatever you're after, Stone, I'm fresh out. Don't let the door hit you in the ass when you leave."

"Nice to see you, too, Mac," I said.

Mac raised his eyebrows, and his expression changed from disgust to puzzlement. He lifted his nose a bit and sniffed the air. He'd caught a whiff of bay rum.

"What is that you're swimming in?" he said. "You smell like you've spent the night in a house of ill repute."

"I'll have to take your word for it," I said. "I wouldn't know what a house of ill repute smells like."

Mac offered a grunt.

"Try telling that lie under oath," he said.

I sat down in the chair across from him.

"I'm here on business," I said. "I need to speak to one of your houseguests—one Henry Brown."

"Huh. You expect me to swallow that? You must be kidding. You talking about the guy who stabbed that woman? Right. I'm to believe that Brown hired you? No way, peeper. That doesn't wash. Get out of here and quit wasting my time. Roll your hoop down another man's road."

"Brown didn't hire me. I have a client who hired me on behalf of Henry Brown. My client believes Brown is innocent."

"I'm not buying it. Who's your client? Not that I expect you'd tell me."

"A concerned citizen," I said.

"Just as I thought" he said. "That's always the way with you, isn't it? You come waltzing in here and demand this, that, and the other thing and expect me to jump through hoops like a trained seal at the circus, but when I want anything from you, you never give me a thing. You clam up tighter than the Sphinx in Cairo."

I shook my head.

"You're wrong."

"Huh?"

"The Sphinx is not in Cairo," I said. "It's down the road near Giza."

Mac glared at me with wide eyes.

"What difference could that possibly make?" he said.

I shrugged.

"I thought you'd want to know. I wanted to offer you something."

Mac looked down at nothing and mumbled under his breath. Then he looked up.

"You can't talk to Brown," he said. "Brown's not talking to anyone. From what I understand, not even to his lawyer. Also, this lawyer of his says no one goes near Brown, not unless he's in the room to represent him. Is that good enough for you? Now, take a hike."

"Who's the lawyer?"

"I don't remember. Some kid who looks younger than the socks I'm wearing. Fresh out of law school from what I hear. Webber, Webster, something like that. You can ask at the desk."

"Mac, who conducted the investigation?"

"Investigation? What investigation?"

"C'mon, Mac."

"Look, this Brown was seen standing over a corpse with the murder weapon in his hand. Is that good enough for you? He was apprehended by a couple of uniforms and identified by an eyewitness. The boys in blue took statements from the women at the boardinghouse. All the women had seen Brown with the victim on earlier occasions. Brown has refused to speak. He knows he's guilty."

"How about the time of day? Does it strike you as odd that someone would commit murder at that particular hour, at the crack of dawn, just when everyone in the place was waking up?"

"What are you talking about?"

"The landlady discovered him a few moments before the alarm clocks went off. Brown woke up the dog and the landlady just as the boarders were coming awake. That's sloppy planning. It seems to me that a safer hour to commit a crime would be at three or four in the morning while everyone was sound asleep."

"So, it wasn't premeditated. He acted rashly, unreasonably. He's guilty, Stone. Leave it alone."

I rose from the chair.

"One last thing, Mac. Which of your boys in blue questioned the women at the boardinghouse? Was it the same cops who nabbed the suspect or was it someone else?"

"I don't want you wasting city personnel's time with your questions," he said.

"C'mon, Mac, play nice. Be a sport. You're always accusing me of taking some poor sap's dough and then bumbling around and making a mess of things. Put yourself in my shoes, my gumshoes if you prefer. All I want to do is ask a few questions. The sooner you tell me who it is, the sooner I'll be out of your office."

Mac scowled.

"Sergeant Holliday was the senior man. Now, get out."

"Always a pleasure, Mac. Like a breath of fresh air which is a rare commodity in this place, I might add."

Mac removed the cigar from his mouth and blew smoke in my direction.

"Get out," he said.

He was beginning to sound like a broken record. I went out and closed the door behind me. Mac never scored high points in tact or diplomacy, but then again, he wasn't running for mayor, either. He was a good cop, and over the years we'd developed a grudging respect for one another even though he enjoyed giving me a hard time. He talked tough, but it was mostly bark. He'd backed me on more than one occasion, and I'd been there for him once or twice myself.

The aroma of coffee wafted down the hallway. I reached an open doorway and saw a cop I didn't recognize. He wore a uniform and poured himself a cup of coffee. He replaced the pot and nodded at me.

"Smells good," I said. "Do you mind?"

"Help yourself, if you've got the stomach."

The room was furnished with a long wooden table that may have arrived on the Mayflower. Its edges were scarred by the burns of dozens of neglected cigarettes. Eight chairs, all empty, were situated around the table. The coffee pot and fixings sat on a counter between a sink and stove. I picked up a cup and rinsed it in the sink and poured some coffee. I winced when I tasted it and wondered if it had been brewed with muddy river water.

"Say, I just left McCormick's office," I said, "and he told me to see Sergeant Holliday. Is he around?"

The cop raised his eyebrows.

"Who are you?" he said.

I introduced myself and gave him a card.

"I need to speak to the sergeant about a case."

He looked skeptical. He looked me over and flicked my card with his thumbnail.

"Have a seat," he said. "I'll see if he's in."

He left the room and about ten minutes later another man in uniform entered.

"I'm Holliday," he said. "What's this about? McCormick didn't say anything to me about talking to a private eye."

I told Holliday who I was and why I was investigating the Cleveland murder case.

"Case?" he said. "What case? There ain't no case. This guy Brown stabbed the woman. She took a knife right in the chest. A witness eyeballed the culprit. We apprehended him. We locked him up. Case closed."

"You mean an eyewitness saw him leave the premises. She didn't see him commit the crime. Look, I'm not questioning your work," I said. "I've spoken to the landlady, and she told me that the police took Miss Cleveland's personal effects. I was just wondering if you picked up any reading or writing material, any books, magazines, maybe a diary."

"Yeah, we took what she had, but there wasn't anything like that in her stuff. A Bible as I recall. Not much else. Just clothing and makeup, that sort of thing. She didn't have much."

He glanced at a clock on the wall.

"Look, if that's all you wanted, I've got to get back to work. Nice talking to you."

I didn't think he meant it. He turned and went out the door. I poured my coffee down the sink. Maybe it would find its way back to the river.

The desk sergeant gave me the name and number of Henry Brown's lawyer, Joseph Webster, with the firm of Hill, Blankenship, and Derby, Attorneys at Law. I wrote down the name and muttered under my breath. The last thing I needed to deal with before the opening game of the World Series was a freshly-minted lawyer. I needed help, and I knew just who to call.

A Good Attorney
A Good Attorney

"My, don't you look handsome?" Agnes said when I came through the door. "You smell nice, too."

"There's at least one detective lieutenant in this city who'd disagree with you on that," I said.

"Oh, pshaw to your stuffy old Lieutenant McCormick. Let him suck sour grapes. What does he know? Say, Ralph Waldo called earlier. He said you'd been asking after him. Is that right? He asked me to call him back when you returned to the office."

"Swell. Call him and ask him to come in as soon as possible," I said. "I need to make some calls from my office."

I poured myself a cup of coffee and went into my office. Agnes had placed some opened mail on my desk along with checks that required my signature. I set the stack of paper aside and reached for the telephone and dialed a number. I lit a cigarette while I waited for a voice on the other end.

"Simon and Simon, Attorneys at Law. How can I help you?"

"Pete Stone for Harry Simon, please."

"One moment."

Harold Simon was my attorney. He and his brother Gerald ran a law firm together. The Simon brothers, Harold and Gerald, aka Harry and Gerry, had more than once come to my defense and saved my backside when I'd crept too far over the legal line in the sand. I'd heard all the lawyer jokes and laughed at a few of them myself, but when you were in a tight spot, there was no better friend than a good attorney. I'd been in tight spots, and the Simon brothers had been there for me. I considered them friends.

"This is Harold Simon."

"Pete Stone, Harry."

"How are you, Pete?"

Harry and I shared amenities, bantered a bit and talked a little baseball before we turned to business.

"Harry, what can you tell me about a lawyer named Joseph Webster?" I said. "Works for Hill, Blankenship, et cetera. Do you know him?"

"Met him once at a Rotary meeting," Harry said. "Don't really know him. He's as wet behind the ears as the ink on his law degree. Young and eager but personable enough, I suppose. Why?"

I filled Harry in on my conversation with Lieutenant McCormick that morning and my desire to visit with Henry Brown. Harry knew what I needed before I asked for it.

"Let me give Webster a call," Harry said. "I'll get back to you."

I thanked Harry and hung up the phone. I picked up the phone again and started to dial another number, but I heard the outer door open and the sound of Agnes's voice followed by another voice I recognized. I replaced the telephone receiver and went into the outer office.

Ralph Waldo had come in wearing a grin and sporting a trim mustache, a new addition since I'd last seen him. He also wore a tan, double-breasted suit over a striped shirt and matching foulard tie, brogue Oxford shoes, and a brown fedora.

"You're looking prosperous, Ralph," I said.

"You look very handsome," Agnes said.

"I thank you for the handsome remark, Miss Agnes," Ralph said and removed his hat, "but the jury's still out on my prosperity," he said to me. "Detecting crime is a hungry business."

"Welcome to the world of the private detective," I said. "Some days you make a buck, some days you don't. Either way, prosperity always lurks just out of reach, around the next corner or over the next hill."

Ralph Waldo had worked for me on an earlier case, before he was a licensed detective. I hired him to be a listener, a gatherer of information, an invisible man. He'd done well working for me, uncovering key information in a case that brought a killer to justice. In the course of that investigation, he'd demonstrated poise and kept a cool head in a crisis. He'd taken a life, but his action had saved mine. After that experience, I wasn't sure if Ralph would want anything to do with the detective business, but he'd surprised me by getting his license and becoming a gumshoe. He had feared his dark skin would lead to doors being slammed in his face, and I assured him that would happen. I also assured him that he would get through other doors that remained closed to me. That's why I'd asked him to come by and see me. We went into my office and sat down.

Ralph was familiar with the news reports of the murder of Rosemary Joy Cleveland. I told him about my visit with Miss Edna at her boardinghouse and my frustration at not being allowed to talk to the other boarders.

"The other women might not want to talk to me, anyway, even if Miss Edna allowed it. I think you'll have better luck with them, Ralph. Miss Edna told me that Rosemary Joy was quiet, withdrawn, and kept to herself. She didn't share much personal information with others. Fair enough, but I'd bet she had a confidant, someone to share her private thoughts and dreams. See if you can find that person, Ralph. See what you can find out."

Ralph agreed to give it a try and wrote down the address of the boardinghouse. He tucked his notepad into his jacket, and I noticed the cover of a book peeking out of his inside pocket.

"What are you reading?" I said.

Ralph followed my eyes to his pocket, and he pulled out a book and placed it on my desk. It was a paperback, fifty pages or so, titled *The Negro Motorist Green-Book*. I thumbed through its pages and scanned listings and advertisements for hotels, restaurants, service stations, auto repair, entertainment, and so forth.

"I've never seen this before," I said. "What is it?"

"It hasn't been out long," Ralph said. "It's a guidebook. That's the second edition. The first copy was printed last year. Most of the listings are for places near New York City, but they've added more businesses across the country, and they'll be adding more next year, too."

"And the advertisements?" I said.

"Those are for establishments that cater to the Negro. Places that folks like me can visit and patronize with no fear of being turned away—or thrown out. Cuts down on the hassles and the violence. Colored folks who travel on the road are starting to carry copies of the Green-Book with them wherever they go. Me, too. Sometimes my business takes me out of town."

I handed the book back to Ralph. It had been over seventy years since the Civil War ended, three generations, and the American Negro still had to learn which doors were open to him and which remained closed. Change never came easy. We said our goodbyes, and he nodded to Agnes as he left. After the door closed, Agnes handed me a note.

"Harry Simon called," she said.

The note was brief.

"Joseph Webster will meet you at the jailhouse at three p.m. today."

I glanced at the Seth Thomas Banjo clock hanging on the wall and saw that it was nearly three already. The eggs I'd eaten that morning were a distant memory, but lunch would have to wait. I told Agnes I'd see her the next morning and left for the police station.

Beer, Tobacco and Peanuts

Joseph Webster's billing was accurate. Everything about him suggested youth and freshness. His suit was pressed, his shoes were shined, and his dark hair was slicked straight back. A prominent Adam's apple bobbed above a knotted tie. I was confident that the next stain Webster got on that tie would be its first. We shook hands, and I was pleased at his firm grip and confident gaze.

"Brown hasn't said much to me," he said. "He seems resigned to his fate."

A uniformed cop ushered us into an interrogation room with gray painted walls and a cement floor. Henry Brown sat at a metal table wearing faded dungarees and a gray shirt. His hands were cuffed. Two empty chairs had been placed on the other side of the table. There was no other furniture in the room. Webster and I each took a chair, and the cop left and closed the door behind him. The audible clicks of the lock echoed in the room and accented its dismal ambience.

"Henry, this man is Mr. Pete Stone," Webster said. "He's a private detective. He's been hired to investigate your case. It would benefit you to speak to him."

Henry Brown said nothing, but he did look in my direction.

"Mr. Brown, may I call you Henry?" I said. Brown remained silent, so I continued. "I've been hired by someone who believes in your innocence, or at least he believes you might be innocent. He's asked me to investigate this matter and see if I can uncover something, anything that might suggest he's right."

Brown stared at the table.

"Who is this someone who hired you?" he said.

"I'm not at liberty to say," I said. "However, whatever happens, whether I find new evidence or not, you must understand that my client has your best interests in mind."

"This client of yours," Brown said. "He another white guy? Like you?" He jutted his chin toward Webster. "Like him?"

"Does that matter," I said, "if he's trying to help you?"

"White man arrested me. White man locked me up. White man gonna try me, and white man gonna hang me. That's all there is to it," he said.

"You may be correct, Henry, but you don't have to make it so easy for them. Tell us what happened. Tell us why it happened. Tell us something."

Brown continued to stare at the table. I lit a cigarette and offered one to him. He shook his head. I decided to try a different approach.

"Peanut," I said. "Why Peanut? Why did Rosemary Joy call you Peanut?"

For the first time since we'd entered the room, Henry Brown looked up and showed a spark of what may have been life in his eyes.

"Who told you that?" he said. "Who told you Rosemary Joy used that name with me?"

"Doesn't matter," I said. "I told you I'm an investigator. I ask questions. People give me answers. Why Peanut?"

Brown gazed ahead at nothing.

"From when we were kids. She called me that years ago."

Kids? That was news. No one had mentioned that Rosemary Joy Cleveland and Henry Brown had known each other when they were kids. Brown continued his unfocused gaze, and I remained silent. Thankfully, so did Webster. I mentally gave the young lawyer points for knowing when to keep his mouth shut.

"It was nothing," Brown said. "Just a nickname I picked up way back. We'd go into town, Rosemary Joy and me. We might sell a few eggs, a gallon of milk, maybe a little honey at the community store. The owner, a kindly old gentleman."

Henry paused and went silent for a moment before gathering his thoughts and continuing.

"He passed not long ago. He would give us a fair price for our goods, then he'd allow us choose a small treat. Rosemary Joy, she'd pick out a jawbreaker or a sucker, something for her sweet tooth, you know, but not me. I'd dip my hand into that peanut barrel and bring out whatever my small fist could hold. I did love them peanuts. Yes, sir. She would laugh at me. I enjoyed eating them peanuts. Ate 'em every chance I got. Never did get my fill. Rosemary Joy took to calling me Peanut. The name stuck."

Henry Brown stopped talking and came out of his reverie and looked around at his surroundings. He seemed to recall where he was, and he went silent again. He stared ahead. I glanced over at Webster. His eyes were wide, but he hadn't spoken.

"That's all I have to say about that," Brown said.

No one spoke. We sat in silence. Webster checked his watch, and the click of the locks echoed in the room again. The cop opened the door.

"Time's up, gentlemen."

Webster said goodbye to Brown, but Brown didn't acknowledge either of us. Webster and I left the room, and I signaled to the cop to step outside. Webster moved down the hall, and I whispered to the cop. He shook his head, but when I took out my wallet, he didn't raise an objection. I pressed some bills into his hand, and he looked up and down the hallway. He took the money and nodded.

Outside the police station, Webster and I stood together on the sidewalk.

"That's the most Henry Brown has spoken since I've met him," Webster said.

"I'm not sure if it's important," I said, "but I didn't know his relationship with the victim went back to their childhoods."

"I didn't either," he said. "Why do you think he killed her?"

I gave Webster a harsh look.

"Maybe he didn't do it. You're his lawyer," I said. "Have you forgotten he's innocent until proven guilty?"

The young man looked sheepish.

"You're right," he said. "Sorry. Say, what was that back there with the policeman? Did I see you slip him some money?"

"Couple of bucks," I said. "It was nothing."

"Yeah, but why? What did you give him the money for?"

Now, it was my turn to feel sheepish.

"The money was for peanuts. I asked him to run out and buy some peanuts for one of his prisoners," I said.

Tom was behind the bar working the stick when I walked in. He gave me a nod and placed a glass under the tap and filled it to the brim with cold Storz beer. I took a stool at the end of the bar, and Tom laid a coaster down in front of me and centered the foamy glass atop it. I thanked him, and when he moved away to service another customer, I spun the stool around and took in the room.

Tom's Inn brought back childhood memories of visiting the tavern each afternoon after my dad had finished his labors. As a youngster, it was my chore to fetch his daily refreshment. Tom returned and asked for a light. I spun the stool back around and lit his cigarette and one for myself.

"You look lost in thought," he said. "What's on your mind?"

"Childhood memories. Did I ever tell you how much I enjoy a good bar?" I said.

"Once or twice."

"Well, I do. The sounds. The smells. The scents of beer, tobacco, and peanuts. The rough language and the good-natured bantering. Simple pleasures. I savored them as a kid and still do today. Dad would come home from work, and I'd grab the pail and hightail it to the bar. The bartender greeted me each day with the same line, 'Hey, kid, how's your old man?' and I'd answer, 'Swell,' and maybe one or two of dad's pals would give me a, 'hello' or 'hey, kid.' The bartender would fill my pail and add a mark to his tally sheet, and out the door I'd hustle, careful not to slosh the brew over the rim of the pail."

"Nice memories, but you'd better be careful," he said. "You're starting to show your age. You sound like me, or worse yet, my old man."

I had to grin, and Tom did, too. He was easily two decades older than I was. Tom and his wife, Mabel, ran a tavern much like the one from my childhood memories. The mahogany bar itself was a gift from the Storz Brewery in exchange for a promise to keep their beer on tap. A few booths ran along the opposite wall, and tables and chairs filled the open floor space. Beyond the bar, toward the back, aromas and sounds came from Mabel's kitchen. Together they ran a nice, cozy, neighborhood inn. I cracked a couple of peanuts and popped the morsels into my mouth and thought about Henry Brown biding time in his cell.

I finished the glass of beer, and Tom replaced it with a fresh one. A couple of guys in soiled khakis sat side-by-side down the bar, and a mix of blue-collared and white-collared patrons sat at tables. Tom filled their glasses and emptied their ashtrays and worked his way back to my end of the bar.

"Busy," he said. "Something to eat?"

I remembered that I hadn't eaten since breakfast.

"Anything sounds good. Ask Mabel to surprise me."

Tom walked back to the kitchen, and a few minutes later Mabel toddled out with a platter in hand. She shuffled toward me as if her feet weighed a ton. They didn't break contact with the floor. Her frame swayed side to side, and the gray bun on her head rocked back and forth. She smiled when she saw me, but fatigue showed through her smile.

"How's my sweetheart?" I said. "You ready to leave this bum and run away with me?"

"Oh, Pete, I'm afraid my running days are over. You should have asked me twenty years ago. These days I can barely walk."

She placed the platter on the bar, and I admired the cuisine. She had prepared a sandwich of corned beef and sauerkraut on dark rye bread with dill pickle spears and a dollop of spicy mustard. Next to the sandwich lay a generous helping of German potato salad. She waited at my elbow until I sampled her creation.

"This is a feast, Mabel. Thank you, darling. Nothing tastes better than food prepared with love."

She smiled and patted my arm and shuffled back to the kitchen. I turned toward Tom.

"I hope I'm not out of line," I said, "but Mabel doesn't look well. She looks exhausted. How is she, Tom?"

Tom glanced toward the kitchen and ground out the butt of his cigarette in an ashtray. I could see the worry in his face.

"She's slowing down, that's for sure. She's not sleeping well, and she's tired a lot of the time. You see how she shuffles. I ask her to pick up her feet, and she tells me she's too tired to pick up her feet, that it's too much trouble. I try to get her to stay home and rest, but she wonders who's going to run the kitchen. She's right, of course. If she stopped cooking, we'd have to quit serving food. I don't know. Maybe I should close the kitchen, but doing that might kill her anyway. Some days I think I should just find a buyer for the whole kit and caboodle and retire to the rocking chair."

"I'd hate to see that happen," I said. "At least wait till after the World Series is over."

He grinned, and that broke the tension, and we drank beer and smoked cigarettes and ate peanuts and talked baseball. The night grew longer, and then it grew shorter. We said our good-byes, and I drove home to my place on Lewellen.

Three in a Row

Three in a Row

Ralph Waldo got back to me on Friday, three days after we met in my office. In the meantime, I called on Wil Fallon to give him an update on my progress, what little there was. He was in his office with a pair of graduate assistants when I arrived. Fallon appeared to be calmer and less reluctant to introduce me than he had been on my earlier visit, although he gave his students only my name and a vague reference to my occupation.

"Pete Stone, these are two of the department's most promising students, Cynthia Buckman and Arthur Cross, each pursuing graduate degrees. We've just been going over some of their recent research. Our students prepare paper after paper in preparation for a life in academia where they must publish their work to survive. Cynthia, Arthur, Mr. Stone is also conducting some research, albeit nonacademic. If you'll excuse us now, he and I have matters to discuss. Continue what you are doing and get back to me at the beginning of next week. We'll go over your results."

The students gathered their notes, nodded politely, and left the office. They struck me as being young and eager to please. Although we hadn't met on my first visit, I recalled that Fallon had mentioned the name Arthur when talking to the student in the hallway. I figured it was the same student.

After the students left, we turned to the reason I'd come to Fallon's office. As anticipated, the report on my investigation was not promising. I explained to the professor how little I had learned on my visit with Henry Brown. I described Brown's reticence to speak, his resignation to his fate, his belief that people had made up their minds concerning his guilt.

"He's given up," I said. "He feels that he's already been tried and convicted and there's nothing he can do. Admittedly, he's probably correct. As unfair as it is, you seem to be the only person who believes in his innocence."

I also discussed my meeting with his attorney.

"Even he has doubts about Brown's innocence," I said.

"What about you?" Fallon said. "You spoke to the young man. Even if he didn't say much, what are your thoughts? How did he strike you? Is he a killer or another victim? Do you think he is guilty?"

I had anticipated this question, but I hadn't drawn a conclusion. I didn't reply, and Fallon smiled.

"I can tell by your hesitance that you aren't convinced of his guilt either," he said. "You have doubts, too, don't you?"

"I'll admit that the crime doesn't make sense to me," I said. "I don't understand what Brown's motive was, but that's not saying much. Killers don't always have a clear or well-considered motive. I don't know enough about Brown or Miss Cleveland. If the murder was premeditated, it was poorly planned. He could have picked a better time of night or day, a time when he stood less chance of being discovered. But if it was a spontaneous act, what occurred at just before dawn to prompt him to lash out so violently? I don't know. It makes no sense. Still, the evidence against him is overwhelming. We can't overlook the evidence, professor."

"But you aren't convinced he is guilty," Fallon said. "Not a hundred percent, anyway. Something inside you is telling you this can't be right. Hang on to that feeling. Please. Don't give up yet. Keep searching for answers."

"I haven't given up," I said, "but I think you're wasting your money."

"I appreciate your candor," he said, "but let me worry about the money."

I told Fallon about bringing Ralph Waldo on board and about his search for someone who knew Rosemary Joy at the boardinghouse.

"Maybe he'll have better luck than I did in talking to the boarders. He might find someone who was close to Miss Cleveland, who can tell us more than the landlady did."

I assured him I'd keep him informed and left his office.

The World Series opened at Yankee Stadium, and the home team had little trouble dispatching the visiting Giants in the first two contests, winning each game with identical scores of eight runs to one.

A sizable crowd gathered each afternoon at Tom's Inn on Seneca to listen to the games, cheer for a favorite team, and kibitz and argue over close calls, pitching match-ups and the strategies of the managers, Joe McCarthy and Bill Terry. The atmosphere was rowdy but good-natured. Tom and Mabel made a few changes to their establishment and its menu in recognition of the fall classic. The radio above the bar was tuned to NBC, and patrons listened to games called by sportscasters, Red Barber, Tom Manning, and Warren Brown. You had to lean in to hear the broadcast over the cheers and heckles from the crowd. You could get anything you wanted from Mabel's kitchen as long as it was a hotdog, and Tom kept the tap flowing with Storz beer. Bowls of peanuts were scattered on tables and strewn along the bar. Empty peanut shells crunched beneath the soles of shoes. Tom sold cigars at a special price of two for a nickel, and trays filled quickly with ashes and butts. Overhead fans struggled to clear the smoky air and failed miserably. It was a great atmosphere and a great week to spend in a saloon.

Friday's game took place at the Polo Grounds. The Giants were looking for some payback in front of a home crowd, but a payback wasn't in the cards. The Yankees scored one run in the second inning and added two more runs in the third when Bill Dickey belted a triple to bring Lou Gehrig home and then scored on a single by George Selkirk. The score was three to nothing in favor of the Yankees when Ralph Waldo walked into the inn. He stepped over the threshold and paused to allow his eyes to adjust to the dim lighting and the smoky air. I called out his name, and he found me at the bar. Tom had a mug of beer waiting for him, but the stools were filled.

"C'mon, Ralph. Let's find a table in the back."

We moved to an empty booth along the rear wall, and Ralph started right in.

"You were right," he said. "Four women left the boardinghouse after the murder. I talked to the three ladies still rooming there without much trouble, but it took me a couple of days to track down the other four who left."

Ralph took a bite out of a hotdog and wiped mustard off the corner of his mouth with a napkin.

"Most of what I learned wasn't useful," he said. "They all knew the Cleveland woman, of course, but not one of them was what you might call close to her. They said she was friendly and pleasant and all, but reserved and private, too. I thought I'd struck out, wasted my time and your money, but the last gal I spoke to was kind of cute, so I asked her to join me for a cup of coffee. We were sitting in this diner, getting to know each other, and suddenly she gets this look and says, 'Wait a minute. I just remembered.' I kept my mouth shut while she gathered her thoughts, and then she tells me about this other woman, a friend of Cleveland's, who came to visit her one Sunday. She didn't listen to what they talked about, but the two of them were huddled together chatting and laughing for most of the afternoon. She said Rosemary Joy was more talkative that day than she'd ever seen her before."

A roar went up at the bar. The Giants had finally scored a run. Tom came over with two fresh glasses of beer and set them on the table.

"Good work," I said. "Have you located the friend?"

"I know where she is, but I haven't spoken to her. After she left that Sunday, Rosemary Joy talked to the others about her. Her name was Ida Mae Parsons. They'd met in school and took some classes together, but Ida Mae didn't finish at Wichita University. Instead, she transferred to the Kansas State Teachers College in Emporia. She was visiting friends in Wichita when she came to the boardinghouse, but she still takes classes and lives in Emporia. I don't know her address. Do you want me to go up there and find her, ask her some questions?"

I made notes in my book and shook my head.

"No, thanks," I said. "I'll go to Emporia. You've done good work, Ralph. I'll take it from here. Is there anything else?"

Ralph read over his notes.

"Yeah, she works off campus, at least she did a couple of months ago, at the Red X Pharmacy on Commercial. Part time, I suppose."

I noted this and nodded.

"I'll run up there tomorrow. See what I can find out. Thanks, again, Ralph."

Ralph gave me a grin.

"I was hoping you'd say that. I really didn't want to drive to Emporia tomorrow," he said.

"Let me guess," I said. "You and your coffee date hit it off. She found you to be smooth, witty, and charming, so you asked her out, and she agreed. Dinner and dancing Saturday night? Am I close?"

He kept his silly grin and tapped the tip of his nose with his finger.

"Hey, Ralph, no one said detecting couldn't be fun," I said.

We hoisted our beers in a toast. Mabel shuffled from the kitchen with another platter of hotdogs, and I caught Tom eyeing her. He looked concerned. Mabel seemed to be moving even slower than the last time I'd seen her. She seemed too exhausted to lift her feet. Ralph and I each ate another hotdog and smoked cigars and listened to Red Barber call the last couple of innings. The Giants didn't score again, and the Yankees won the third game by a score of five to one. That made it three in a row for the boys from the Bronx. One more victory, and the series crown would be theirs.

Back Roads and Baseball
Back Roads and Baseball

Emporia lay ninety miles or so to the north and east of Wichita. As I drove through the Flint Hills, I realized there were worse ways to spend a morning. Time behind the wheel of my car was time to think. I've always turned to back roads and baseball for answers to life's riddles. I drove with the top up on the roadster and admired the rolling terrain and the tall prairie grass gone yellow, and I pondered how Henry Brown, Peanut, could have committed such a heinous crime as murder. I had plenty of time to ponder the question but not enough time to come up with an answer. The miles rolled by until the outline of buildings broke the horizon.

The community of Emporia was home to some fourteen thousand people along with the Kansas State Teachers College where Ida Mae Parsons took classes. It was a Saturday, and I doubted I would find her on campus. Before searching for her home address, I intended to ask for her at the pharmacy where she worked part time. College students who held down jobs often worked on the weekends.

I came in from the west side of the city and drove east on Sixth Street toward downtown. Pickup trucks and cars rolled along the thoroughfare, driven by residents who lived and worked in the community and farmers who came to town on the weekend to do their trading. When I reached the center of town at Commercial Street, I turned left and pulled up in front of a building with an Art Deco façade and a sign over the door that read Red X Pharmacy. Pedestrians in suits and dresses and khakis and overalls strolled on the walkways.

A bell tinkled when I opened the door to the drugstore, and I sensed movement toward the back. A male voice called out, "Be right with you." Merchandise displays lined the walls. Toiletries, candies, writing supplies, tobacco products and dozens of other items filled the showcases toward the front with medicinal products offered toward the back of the store. Shelves were crowded but neatly arranged. A ceiling fan hummed overhead.

"How can I help you?"

The man who spoke wore a shirt and tie beneath a white bib apron. He identified himself as Joe Kowalski, proprietor, and I introduced myself and gave him a card.

"I understand that Miss Ida Mae Parsons works for you, or at least she did recently. I'd like to speak with her."

He read my card, pursed his lips, and frowned.

"A private investigator from Wichita. This has something to do with the murder of her friend, I suppose."

So, Ida Mae Parsons did work at the pharmacy. Good.

"Yes," I said. "I'd like to ask her a few questions."

He frowned again.

"She's been awfully upset since the news. I hate to get her worked up again. It may be none of my business, but why is a private detective all the way from Wichita here in my store asking questions? The police never came up here, at least they never came to my store, and Ida Mae never mentioned talking to the police."

"The police have their suspect behind bars. There was no reason for them to talk to Miss Parsons. I'm working on another angle."

I looked around the store. No employees were in sight.

"If Miss Parsons isn't here," I said, "maybe you could tell me where to find her."

A muffled sound of movement came from behind the rear wall.

"She's in back," Kowalski said, "counting inventory. I'll tell her you're here, but she may not want to talk to you. Like I said, she's been upset over this."

He disappeared for a moment and returned with a young woman walking behind him. She seemed reluctant to speak, but her voice was strong and clear.

"I'm Ida Mae. Mr. K. said you wanted to speak to me."

I introduced myself and explained I had come to Emporia to investigate the death of Rosemary Joy Cleveland. She listened patiently to what I said.

"I'd like to talk to someone who knew Miss Cleveland. I understand you were her friend. Will you talk to me?"

She shifted from one foot to the other and glanced at a clock on the wall.

"I go to lunch in forty minutes. I could see you then I suppose."

"Perfect," I said. I'd noticed a diner at the other end of the block and asked her to meet me there. She agreed.

The diner had a few late morning customers, but the lunch crowd hadn't arrived yet. Folks sipped coffee or munched on a doughnut or a sandwich. I took a booth in the rear and ordered coffee and asked the waitress to leave menus for two. I opened a copy of the Wichita newspaper I'd brought from home and lit a cigarette. I glanced at the headlines and a voice interrupted me.

"Howdy, stranger. Welcome to our fair city."

I closed my newspaper and looked up at the face of a man I recognized, even though I'd never met him. He looked at my newspaper, and I rose out of my seat and shook his hand.

"Wichita is a fine town, but we're proud of Emporia, too, you know."

An elderly gentleman, he appeared to be in his late sixties or early seventies. A broad smile beamed over his dimpled chin. He wore a gray suit and a bow tie.

"Here," he said. "As long as you're visiting our community, you should read what we have to say."

He handed me a copy of the local newspaper and tipped his hat and walked away, shaking hands and chatting with other patrons before leaving the diner. Of course, the local folks all knew William Allen White, the renowned owner and editor of *The Emporia Gazette*. I'd seen his picture in the papers and read about him more than once.

I skipped over the national news and scanned the local columns and advertisements. The Saint Joseph Church in Olpe was to host a benefit chicken dinner on Tuesday, all you could eat for forty cents. The local college Hornets had stung the Yellowjackets of Superior State Teachers College the evening before by the score of 26 to 7. I speculated the return trip to northern Wisconsin would be long and subdued for the losers. The latest Oldsmobile models had arrived at Davis-Child Motors. *Thunder in the City* with Edward G. Robinson was playing at the Strand Theater while the Granada was showing *100 Men and a Girl* with Deanna Durbin. The Tom Mix Circus had performed at the Fowler Grounds that week, and the Red X Pharmacy ran an advertisement for roll-your-own tobacco products. I turned to the back page, and a figure slipped into the booth across the table from me.

"I hope I'm doing the right thing," Miss Parsons said. "I don't know if I should be talking to you or not."

"Why not? Why shouldn't you be talking to me?"

The waitress arrived and took our orders. We each settled on a grilled cheese sandwich with tomato soup. Ida Mae ordered a glass of milk, and I had more coffee.

"Are you afraid of something?" I asked.

"Maybe. I really don't know. I feel something, but I'm not sure it's fear. I can't explain it."

"Let's just talk," I said. "Tell me about yourself."

Ida Mae had met Rosemary Joy at the university in Wichita. They were assigned as lab partners in a biology class and soon developed a friendship that extended beyond the classroom. They had different majors, but they took classes together when they could. They studied together and ate meals together and shopped together. The waitress arrived with our food, but Ida Mae continued talking.

"We probably would have shared an apartment, but Rosemary Joy often lived with the folks she cared for, even before she graduated. We saw each other often, though."

"I understand Rosemary Joy loved literature. She enjoyed reading. Is that true?"

"Oh, yes, she read all the time. Good literature, classic literature. Dickens and Austen and poets, too. She was a reader."

"Did she own many books? None was found in her room at the boardinghouse."

"No, I don't think so. The books I recall her reading came from the library. She didn't have money to buy books."

"Did she write? Keep a diary?"

Ida Mae nodded.

"Yes, yes, she kept a diary. Wrote in it every night, too, she told me, but always when she was alone. Didn't tell me anything else about it, though. Those were her most private thoughts, I guess. We were friends, sure, but her diary belonged to her and her alone."

I made a mental note. Cleveland had kept a diary, but no diary had been recovered by the police.

"Sounds like you were close," I said. "You must have met Henry Brown."

"Peanut? Sure, I knew Peanut. Lots of times we'd be together, all three of us laughing or eating, maybe going to a movie."

Her face broke into a grin that disappeared in an instant. She stopped talking and sipped her milk. We ate in silence for a few moments. Ida Mae kept her eyes on her food and didn't look at me until I spoke.

"I'm looking for the truth, Ida Mae, the truth. The police have their version of the truth. They have their suspect behind bars. If Brown is the killer, you have nothing to fear. He'll be tried and convicted and probably hanged. All of this will be over. That is if he is the killer. If he's not the killer, then the killer is still free, still out there somewhere. I've met with Brown, and he wouldn't say much to me. He hasn't said much to anyone since his arrest. However, I should tell you that not everyone is convinced of his guilt. My client, the man who hired me, believes that Brown is innocent. That's why I'm here. That's why I located you, to see what you know about Henry Brown and Miss Cleveland, to see if the police do have the right man behind bars."

Ida Mae's eyes grew round.

"You mean someone else thinks Peanut is innocent?" she said.

"Someone else?" I said. "Are you telling me that you think Brown is innocent, also?"

She didn't speak.

"That's why you're afraid, isn't it?" I said. "You think someone else murdered your friend, and if you're right, that murderer may come after you, too."

It took a moment for Ida Mae to reply, but I remained silent. Finally, she nodded.

"I can't believe that Peanut killed her. He loved his Rosemary Joy. He looked after her. He cared for her, and she cared for him."

"I understand that they knew each other from the time when they were children," I said, "but they didn't have a romantic relationship. Is that correct?"

Ida Mae's brow furrowed, and she looked puzzled.

"I thought you knew. Are you saying you don't know?" she said.

"Know what?" I said.

She looked down at the table and shook her head, then she looked at me.

"Peanut Brown and Rosemary Joy," she said. "They were brother and sister."

I've Been Fortunate

"**P**rofessor Fallon, this is your last chance. Tell me the whole truth. All of it. You've been holding back since you first telephoned me and I agreed to take on this investigation. You've given me bits and pieces but not the whole picture. What you've given me is true—I don't doubt that, but there's more. You haven't told me everything. You're going to tell me now. I'm through chasing my tail and jumping through hoops."

My words were harsh. I intended them to be. It was Sunday evening. Fallon and I were in his study at his home, and I was irate. It had been a long weekend. I was tired and short on patience. I had returned to Wichita from Emporia on the previous evening. I'd called the Fallon home and spoken to his wife. She explained that her husband was delivering a paper at an educational conference in Kansas City, and she expected him to return home Sunday evening. I told her it was important that I see Dr. Fallon as soon as possible, and she invited me to come to their home at eight o'clock on Sunday.

I had spent Sunday afternoon at Tom's Inn where we chatted and bickered over sports with other wannabe athletes of days gone by. Wichita University's football team had trounced Kansas University 18-7 the day before, so we toasted that victory.

We had listened to Red Barber on the radio and celebrated the final game of the World Series. The Giants took the fourth game on Saturday, but the Yankees countered with their ace, Lefty Gomez, on the mound for game five on Sunday. Myril Hoag and Joe DiMaggio each homered for the Yankees to give them an early two-run lead, but Mel Ott tied the game with a homer for the Giants in the third inning. Gomez and Lou Gehrig each drove in a run later in the game to put the Yankees ahead 4 to 2. That score held, and the Yankees won the game and the World Series, four games to one.

Raucous laughter and back-slapping in the bar rose to a crescendo and then ebbed and died away. Men sighed and cleared their throats and gazed into their beers and pondered the dark days fallen upon us. The last pitch of the season. The last crack of the bat. The final roar of the crowd. It would be another six months before horsehide smacked a mitt or cracked a bat, before hearts that loved the game would beat again.

After the game ended and the crowd cleared, I had coffee and quiet conversation with Tom. Peanut shells cluttered the floor. Empty beer glasses stood on the bar, and cigar butts smoldered in the ashtrays. Litter and emptiness were all that remained of the week's hoopla. Mabel had closed the kitchen and gone home to rest. She hunched over and shuffled her feet as she went out the door. Tom and I chatted together and drank coffee until we decided we'd had enough. The clock ticked toward eight and my appointment with Fallon. Tom hung up the closed sign and locked the door.

It was time for me to get back to work. I needed to ask Fallon some questions, and I needed answers. I had left the bar and driven across town and parked in front of a large colonial style structure on Fountain Street near College Hill Park. Fallon's tan Hudson was parked in the driveway.

I rang the bell, and Dr. Fallon opened the door. He led me into a spacious living room with Victorian furnishings and introduced me to his wife, Muriel, who sat in a chair next to a lamp and sipped tea, an open book on her lap. She was an attractive woman who appeared to be much younger than Fallon. He then led me to his study, ushered me in, and closed the door. I waited until we were alone before I delivered my tirade and demanded to hear the whole story.

"This is your last chance," I said.

Fallon maintained a calm demeanor throughout my rant. He gestured toward a pair of chairs.

"Perhaps we should sit down," he said.

We took seats facing each other on either side of a coffee table. I told him about my recent trip to Emporia and my visit with Ida Mae Parsons. When I told him of my discovery that Henry Brown and Rosemary Joy Cleveland were siblings, I was not surprised at his lack of surprise. This was not news to him. I repeated my demand that he tell me everything he knew.

"Yes, you deserve to know, I suppose, but can you promise me that what I tell you will not leave this room?"

"No, I can't make that promise," I said. "What I do promise you is that I won't blab what I hear. I will be discreet, but I won't break the law. If what you tell me has a bearing on this case, on the guilt or innocence of Henry Brown, then I can't promise I'll sit on it. I'll have to tell the police. I will be discreet, but I won't withhold evidence."

Fallon didn't seem satisfied with my answer, but at least he knew where I stood—and where he stood. He rose from his chair and moved to a sideboard and poured brandy into a pair of snifters. He handed one of the snifters to me and lifted the other to his nose and breathed in the aroma.

"This is one of Hennessy's finer labels," he said.

I sniffed the dark amber liquid and took a sip and savored the flavor. It was the best brandy I'd ever tasted, and I told him so.

"I'm glad you like it," he said. "Not everyone has a palate for finer tastes."

"I think I chose the wrong profession," I said. "I never knew that college professors lived like this."

He chuckled.

"Most don't. Teaching at the university has afforded me personal pleasure and satisfaction, and it allows for a comfortable lifestyle. Luxuries are another matter. We in academia struggle for decent wages, especially those beginning their careers. Taxpayers and politicians hold forth on the importance of an education and its necessity to a fulfilled life, and for the most part they believe what they spout. Until it comes time to pay the bills, that is. When compensation of the teachers charged with educating their offspring enters the discussion, both politicians and taxpayers tend to tighten their purse strings and slash budgets. Being an educator brings personal reward, but my salary doesn't pay for luxuries."

He hoisted his snifter.

"Some would say I've been fortunate. Maybe I have been. I'm not ungrateful, but I do wonder. I didn't marry as a young man, and my wife and I have no children. I like children and would enjoy having my own, but that was not to be. There was a time when I thought I'd father several, but no, that time has passed. When my wife and I got married, it was too late in life for me to raise a child, and my wife is not the mothering kind. She was happy to live in a nice home surrounded by comforts, just the two of us. So, we remained childless.

"It's a universal truth that married couples who remain childless accrue more wealth than those who raise families. It only makes sense. Raising children takes money. Accruing wealth is no reason to forgo having children, you understand, but it is often a byproduct of not having children. Are you a father?"

I told him I was.

"Then you know something about the responsibilities that entails. A good father sees that his children are fed, clothed, sheltered and educated. Of course, you know that."

I assured him I did. He rose from his chair and refilled our snifters. Then, he reached above the sideboard and brought out a box of cigars. I raised my eyebrows. I assumed he didn't smoke.

"Surprised?" he said. "I don't often use tobacco. The smoke bothers Muriel's sinuses, so I limit my habit to my study. However, nothing goes better with fine brandy than a good cigar. Try one of these. They're made in the Dominican Republic by the Leon Family."

He lit my cigar and his, and our smoke wafted toward the ceiling fan. Like the brandy I'd been sipping, the cigar was the richest and smoothest I'd ever smoked. I complimented him on his taste. Fallon nodded in appreciation and continued speaking.

"For reasons I will explain, I didn't marry as a young man. I worked hard. I taught students and wrote the requisite academic papers and followed them with a book on Literature of the Midwest that garnered a few accolades. I got published, met the right people, became tenured, and made a name for myself in my little corner of the world. The money wasn't bad considering I had no one to spend it on but myself. So, I invested, primarily in businesses that made their start right here in Wichita, businesses like Coleman Company, NuWay Cafes, Stearman Aircraft, The Mentholatum Company, among others. The companies grew. They've done well, and so have I. I sold some of my holdings in 1929, not long before the crash."

"A lot of smart men didn't sell before the crash," I said. "Did you have a crystal ball or were you just lucky?"

He laughed and said, "A little of each, I suppose. My crystal ball was my barber."

"Excuse me?" I said.

"It was my good fortune to have a casual conversation with my barber. That and having read a book titled *Extraordinary Popular Delusions and the Madness of Crowds*. Are you familiar with it?"

"I recognize the title, but I haven't read it."

"I recommend it. It's a wonderful handbook for eluding the wiles of fortune-tellers, snake oil salesmen, stockbrokers, and fork-tongued politicians. It was written nearly a century ago by a Scotsman named Charles Mackay. People are herd animals, Mr. Stone, and a herd animal feels most vulnerable when alone. It is difficult to act alone. Yet, if the individual seeks safety and peace, he often must ignore the herd, go on his own. Mackay recognized that. He studied that. He looked back at history and documented the instances when herd mentality led to financial and personal ruin for everyone. Did you know that there was a time three hundred years ago when nobles in Europe ransomed their fortunes for a handful of tulip bulbs? Herd mentality. Eventually, of course, the bubble bursts, the music stops, and those left holding the tulip bulbs realize their investment is worthless, and they are left penniless.

"Herd mentality. It's how politicians win office. A herd, a crowd of people, recognize a lie when they hear it once, but when that lie is repeated over and over, again and again, with absolute conviction, the herd begins to believe it, and once they believe it, the herd is lost. They stampede. They rush the liar, the messiah, and throw themselves at his feet and beg for more lies, and the messiah obliges. Only by stepping away from the herd, only by observing the scene apart and from a distance, only by thinking for oneself, can one avoid ruin.

"The words of that book came back to me when I was getting a haircut one day, some eight years ago. It was in the late spring, early summer, I suppose, and my barber started talking about the stock market. He opened up to me about his investments, and he began complaining. He said his portfolio was up only twenty percent over the previous year. Can you imagine hearing those words today? His portfolio was up twenty percent, and the man was dissatisfied! When your barber pontificates on the stock market as if he were a seasoned professional and twenty percent annual returns are no longer satisfactory, it's a signal that a fall in the market is due. The music is about to stop playing. It was time for me to step away from the herd. I called my broker that same day and placed sell orders. Over the next few months, I divested myself of much of my holdings. The crash came in October of 1929, as you well remember. It was inevitable, but I barely felt it. That barber was my crystal ball, he and the book by Charles Mackay. That's how I avoided a huge loss and why I've managed to live well these past years.

"Muriel and I married late. I'm sixty-three now, and she's two decades younger. She had a brief marriage when she was young, but it didn't last. We met at a dinner party and discovered shared loves of literature and the arts. We dated, and we saw each other more and more. One thing led to another, and eventually we were married. Our union has been satisfactory, I suppose. We've found a certain happiness together."

Fallon paused for a long moment before he spoke again. I pondered the nature of his words, a satisfactory union. Its very name sounded unsatisfactory to me.

"What you've been listening to is a summary of my life. I assure you, Mr. Stone, I am not often this verbose, at least when talking about myself. On the contrary, I am a private person. I cherish my privacy. It is only this extraordinary circumstance that leads me to divulge what I have told you. However, I've told you nothing that isn't known to select friends who know me well. What I am about to tell you now is not known, however, neither to my friends nor to my wife. I must ask you to respect my wishes and keep what I say between us. It must not leave this room."

"Once again, professor, if what you tell me is not relevant to the case, I will not talk about it."

"Yes, yes, so you've said. I'll have to accept your terms, I suppose. As I've told you, my wife and I married late. As you may well assume, Muriel was not my first love. I fell in love years earlier as a younger man. I hadn't known many women. Too busy with my work. The woman I loved was in her late twenties. I was a few years older. She was a returning student who left school earlier to earn money to pay for her education. I was one of her teachers. She may have been the only woman I ever truly loved. However, she was a student, and I was a teacher. A student-teacher romance spells doom. Faculty members are cautioned against it. Classroom relationships are verboten at the university. That said, they are also as common as chalk dust in the air. We were consenting adults, but had our relationship been discovered, she would have been expelled, and my academic career would have been over. I would have been banned from the campus. We were young and foolish. We loved each other, and we continued seeing each other. Inevitably, she got pregnant."

He paused to sip his brandy and puff on his cigar and continued.

"I asked her to marry me. She refused. She knew a marriage between us would never work, would ruin both our lives. She was right, of course, but at that point I didn't care. I loved her, and I knew I'd love our child. I had fathered a child, and I wanted to be a father to that child. She was determined, however. She would not allow this episode to ruin our lives. So, she broke it off with me. She left. She left the university. She left me."

Fallon sipped brandy and blew smoke from his cigar and stared at the ceiling and gathered his thoughts.

"People often get pregnant before their wedding day," I said. "It's not the end of the world. It doesn't ruin lives. Why did she think your lives would be ruined if you got married? Simply because she was one of your students?"

Fallon brought his gaze back to me and shook his head.

"No, it was more than that. We were too unlike one another. We came from different backgrounds. We came from different families, different people. Our differences would have led to our being scorned by society. Society would have turned its back on us."

He paused again, and I waited.

"You see, I was a Caucasian, but she was a Negro."

I'd always been a lousy poker player. I'd never developed a good poker face. My face was too easy to read. Fallon caught my expression and smiled. I realized where this conversation was headed.

"I think you understand now," he said. "As I say, she left. It was her wish that we stop seeing each other, so, I obliged. We stopped seeing each other. She had the baby on her own. It was a boy."

Here it comes, I thought. He looked at me and nodded.

"That's right," he said. "Henry Brown is my son."

Rosemary Joy Kept a Diary
Rosemary Joy Kept a Diary

O ur brandy glasses were empty, but we'd had enough to drink. The remains of our cigars lay in the ashtray. A clock chimed from another room. Fallon's wife knocked softly on the door and announced that she was going to bed. I lit a cigarette. I didn't want to leave. I had questions.

"When I first met you," I said, "you told me you had never met Henry Brown. You said you'd never spoken to the man."

"And I told you the truth. I have never met nor spoken to Henry Brown. That was his mother's wish, a wish I have honored."

There was more. I waited for him to continue.

"When the baby was born, Joy listed the father as deceased on the birth certificate. That was her name, Joy—Joy Brown. She gave her last name to her son. She left the university, but she remained in Wichita. Early on, I tried to communicate with her, an attempt to maintain a relationship with her, with both her and her son, but she refused to see me or talk to me. She thought it would be easier on all of us to sever our relationship entirely. She may have been right. It may have been easier, but that didn't mean it was easy. I continued to love her, but I stopped trying to see her and the boy. I sent her a check from time to time, and I was pleased that she cashed them. It was the least I could do.

"Then, she met another man, a man named Cleveland, and they married. They had a child of their own, Rosemary Joy, and Henry now had a younger sister, albeit his half-sister. As far as I know, they had a good life together, the four of them. Our paths didn't cross, as you might imagine. We lived in different neighborhoods, traveled in different circles. I thought of them often, but I had my own life to live. I poured myself into my work. It was the right thing to do. That's what I told myself. Over time, regret and sorrow dissipated into ache, and the ache dulled as years went by. I never got over my feelings for Joy Brown, but I've learned to live with them.

"Then, tragedy struck the family a couple of years ago. Joy and her husband died in an automobile accident. When I heard the news, long buried feelings rose to the surface once again. I thought of her, of us, and what might have been. I thought of Joy's children. They were young adults by then and able to fend for themselves, but the loss they felt must have been tremendous.

"It wasn't until Rosemary Joy enrolled in my class that I met her and saw the boy I had fathered for the first time, always at a distance. Even from a distance, I could tell that he was his sister's guardian, her protector. He isn't a man who would harm his sister. I cannot accept that he would do such a thing. That's it, Mr. Stone. That's everything. I'm convinced Henry Brown is innocent, despite the evidence against him and the police report on the murder. I'm convinced someone else killed that young woman, but I have no proof. That's your job. It's why I hired you. It's up to you to find the proof that Brown is innocent."

I caught Lieutenant McCormick on a good day. He listened to what I had to say without interrupting and didn't bark at me until I finished. Mac always listened well even if he later dismissed what he heard. I told him about my trip to Emporia and my visit with Ida Mae Parsons. I told him what I'd learned about the relationship between Brown and the victim. I told him the story without revealing details that would lead to Fallon's identity. I saw no reason to mention his involvement.

"My client describes Brown as Miss Cleveland's protector. The landlady at the boardinghouse used similar terms. Ida Mae Parsons knew both as well as anyone I've talked to, and she thinks Brown is innocent. She's in fear that the real killer is still on the loose. Mac, they were brother and sister, siblings, for crying out loud."

"Brother and sister, siblings," Mac said. "That proves nothing. The first recorded murder in the history of mankind was between siblings. You're wasting my time."

"Okay, okay, I went to Sunday school, too," I said. "I know the story of Cain and Abel. That was a murder based on jealousy. This is different. These young people lost their parents. All they had was each other. What man kills the only person in the world that belongs to him? It makes no sense."

Mac remained unconvinced.

"According to her friend, Ida Mae, Rosemary Joy kept a diary," I said. "No diary was recovered by the police. Doesn't that sound suspicious?"

"How could I or anyone else on the force know the whereabouts of a diary that may or may not exist? There was no diary in the victim's room. There was no diary on the suspect. The suspect—stop and consider the suspect for a moment. He was witnessed standing over the body with the murder weapon in his hand. He ran when he was discovered. He's said nothing in his defense since he was captured. In fact, he's said almost nothing at all. Does that sound like the behavior of an innocent man to you?"

"It sounds like the behavior of a frightened man," I said, "Look, I've made arrangements to talk to him again. I know someone who might get him to talk, who will at least encourage him to talk."

I glanced at my watch.

"They should be here now," I said.

"What have you got up your sleeve, Stone?"

"Brown won't talk to the police. He clams up with his lawyer. I assured him I was working on his behalf, and he barely acknowledged me, hardly said a word. I've got somebody waiting outside who he may talk to. At least give it a shot, Mac. At least see if he has something to say."

McCormick was reluctant, but we left his office and found Ralph Waldo sitting on a bench near the desk sergeant. A few minutes later, Brown's lawyer, Joseph Webster, came through the door.

"Sorry I'm late. Got held up in court," he said.

McCormick and Ralph knew each other, but Mac knew the lawyer only by name, so I made the introductions.

"This is your plan?" Mac said, nodding toward Ralph.

"Brown is leery of speaking to anyone who is Caucasian, and why wouldn't he be?" I said. "White men have done nothing but hound him since the crime was committed—arrested him, accused him, booked him, and locked him up. Even the men who want to help him are Caucasian. He's scared. Maybe he'll talk to Ralph. Maybe he'll tell Ralph why he did it or at least what he knows about the crime."

Mac didn't look convinced, but the assembly had gathered. He looked over each of us and agreed to let the plan play out. Henry Brown was ushered into an interrogation room and seated at a table. A moment later, Ralph Waldo entered the room and took the empty chair on the other side of the table. The rest of us stood in a darkened room and watched the proceedings through a transparent mirror that allowed us to view the interrogation without being observed by Waldo or Brown. Brown had been told that the conversation would be recorded, and a microphone rested on the table. The microphone also transmitted the conversation into our dark room.

Neither Brown nor Waldo spoke at first. Each man studied the other in silence. Finally, Ralph spoke.

"I'm a detective," Ralph said, "same as the white man who spoke to you earlier. In fact, I sometimes work with that man."

Brown's eyes grew wide.

"You a detective? No, man. I ain't believin' that."

Ralph said nothing. He pulled out his wallet and showed his identification.

"That don't prove nothing," Brown said.

"It's real. You can believe it or not, but it's real. I'm a real detective, and I'm here to help you. They've been telling me you got nothing to say. You're just going to roll over without a word, without a fight. Roll over and die and be done with it. They tell me you're guilty. You killed a young woman, your sister."

Brown's eyebrows went up.

"Yes, that's right," Ralph said. "We know Rosemary Joy was your sister. You could have told us that, saved us a lot of time. How can a man kill his little sister? I've been thinking about that. I haven't come up with an answer, but I've been thinking about that. You won't have long to dwell on that question, though. No, no, not long at all. Things will move quickly now. You'll get a trial, a speedy trial. Then, you'll most likely hang. Yes, sir, you'll hang, and that'll be all she wrote for Henry Brown. That'll be his life story. He lived. He murdered his sister. He was hanged. End of story."

Seconds ticked, and Brown stared into the eyes of Ralph Waldo. His gaze never wavered. He spoke.

"You don't know a damn thing. Why should you care 'bout Henry Brown anyway? What's your stake in this?"

"I'm just a friend of a man who's trying to help you," Ralph said. "I've got no stake in this. And you're right. I don't know a damn thing. The cops don't know a damn thing. Nobody knows a damn thing about this except you, Henry Brown. Only you. And nobody is going to know a thing unless you speak up and say something."

More seconds went by. Brown stared at Ralph Waldo. Then he looked over at the mirror. The corners of his mouth may have gone up a whisper. He looked back at Ralph.

"She was my baby sister. You're right about that. My baby sister. Only everything else you've said, everything else they think they have against me is wrong. I did for my sister. I took care of my sister. I did whatever I could to make her life easier, make it better. She was special. She was smart. She had brains. She read. She knew books and words and such, things I never learned. She took care of people, that's what she did. She cared for people who were too sick or old or feeble to care for themselves. She cared for those folks, so I cared for her.

"I stopped to see her often, wherever she lived. When she lived in the homes of the folks she cared for, I stopped there to see what she needed, a pair of shoes, or a hairbrush, or a coat, you see. She was special, and I wanted her to know she was special."

Brown went silent and stared at the table and gathered his thoughts. He looked up.

"That day, that morning, I went to her room early. She was expecting me. She told me to tap on her window, and then she'd open the back door and let me in. Only when I tapped, she didn't come to the window. I tapped again and again. Nothing. So, I went to the back door, and I saw that the door was open a bit. I went in the boardinghouse. I went to her room which was right near that back door. Her bedroom door was open, too. It wasn't especially cold that morning, but I suddenly got a chill, like my blood had turned to ice. I felt something bad.

"It was still mostly dark outside, and I gazed into the shadows in the room. I whispered her name, Rosemary Joy, and waited to hear her say Peanut, but she didn't speak my name. She didn't call back to me. Maybe she's down the hall in the bathroom, I thought to myself, but already I knew inside of me that something bad had happened. I knew it. I felt it in my heart. I reached for the light switch and turned on the light, and there she was—on the floor, on the floor with that thing, that horrible knife sticking out of her."

Brown paused and choked back his emotion.

"Blood, so much blood, Rosemary Joy's blood, her life pooled around her on that old floor. She'd bled like a slaughtered animal. I gasped and sobbed and screamed, but it didn't matter. She just laid there. I knew she was gone. I heard movement upstairs. Someone was on the stairs. My mind wasn't workin' right. I thought maybe, maybe, if I pulled that knife out of my Rosemary Joy, maybe she'd be right again. Maybe she'd sit up and smile and throw her arms around me and call me Peanut again, you know? So, that's just what I did. I yanked that knife out of my baby sister, and I called out her name, but you know she didn't move. She was dead. I knew it for sure. She was dead. My sister was gone on from this world never to return.

"About that time, this old woman, Miss Edna who ran the place, she came into the room with her big dog, and she let out a wail and pointed her boney finger at me and yelled, 'You did it! You killed her! You did it!' I was surprised to hear that, yes, I was, although looking back on it now, I can understand why she'd think that, me standing there with that knife in my hand and all that blood and all. I was scared. I wasn't thinking right. I just dropped that knife right there, and I lit out the back door, and I ran. I ran, but I had no place to hide. The police found me in no time at all. They locked me up, and here I sit.

"I know the police think I'm guilty, but I'm not. I didn't kill my baby sister, but when the white man gets his mind set on a notion, his mind stays set. No, sir. Like you said, I'm gonna hang, and that's all there is to it. Peanut is fine with that, too. I ain't got a thing to live for. I'm ready to leave this old world and visit my sister in the otherworld. I'm ready to be with my Rosemary Joy. The only reason I'm talking to you here today is because you might see that I'm telling the truth. You might believe me. Nobody in a courtroom will believe me, but you just might. You can't save me, but if you know I'm telling the truth, then maybe you can find the man who killed my baby sister. You do that for me, you hear, detective? You find the man who stuck that knife into my Rosemary Joy. Don't be worrying about me no more. Don't waste your time. Just promise me, promise me now, you hear? Promise me that you'll find that killer."

With that, Brown went silent and stared down at the table. Ralph looked at him for a long moment and rose from his chair and left the room. A uniformed cop entered the room to usher Brown back to his cell. McCormick, Webster, and I exited the dark room and met Ralph in the hallway.

"That boy didn't kill his sister," Ralph said. "You heard what he said. I believe him, too. He isn't capable of making up a lie like that."

"I agree," I said.

"I hope you two find something that will hold up in court," Webster said. "Brown seems sincere to me, but I need proof to sway a judge and jury."

"Now, let's all wait a minute here," Mac said. "Nothing Brown said in there constitutes proof of his innocence. That's just his story. His story, and he's had plenty of time these past few days to dream up a story. Let's don't jump to conclusions."

Ralph looked at Mac and shook his head.

"Brown's right about one thing," he said. "No jury is going to believe him. He's a dead man unless we can find the real killer."

"Real killer, real killer," Mac said. "Listen to yourselves. He's the man who was holding the knife in his hand." Mac turned to me. "By the way," he said, "I had that knife checked for prints, and Brown's prints were the only ones we found."

"Good for you," I said, "but you know that doesn't prove a thing. The killer could've worn gloves."

Mac mumbled something and shook his head.

"You did a great job in there, Ralph," I said. "You're the only person he's opened up to. Thank you."

"What's next?" Ralph said.

"Next, we find the killer," I said.

Detectives Know Everything
Detectives Know Everything

We went back to the beginning, and we worked together. We spoke to Miss Edna, and she recounted the events she witnessed just as she had when we first met. She also confirmed that Henry Brown ran out of the boardinghouse empty-handed. He was not carrying the elusive diary or anything else for that matter.

We canvassed the neighborhood. We knocked on doors and spoke to folks who lived near the boardinghouse, but we came up empty. The crime had been committed in the wee hours when folks were just getting out of bed. No one heard or saw anything unusual that day.

I telephoned Ida Mae Parsons in Emporia to see if she had anything else to offer. Did she recall Rosemary Joy being close to another friend? She knew of no one.

We talked to Rosemary Joy's most recent employer where she had provided daily medical care, and they knew of no one who would harm her. "She was such a kind and caring person," they said. "It makes no sense that someone like her should go this way."

I took Ralph to the university to give our report. Fallon was in his office with a departmental secretary when we called on him. She was sitting in front of his desk taking notes in shorthand. He introduced her as Gertrude O'Neill. She rose and smiled. She closed her notepad and tucked her pencil into her hairdo.

"Congratulations, professor," she said when she left the office. "I think it's just wonderful."

Fallon waved her out the door with a smile.

"Thank you, Gertie," he said.

"Are congratulations in order?" I said.

"Oh, it's nothing. The dean has named me as the new chair of the department. Internal stuff. You're here on business, and I see you've brought someone with you."

I congratulated Fallon on his promotion and introduced Ralph Waldo. They shook hands, and we all sat down. I gave Fallon a brief report. I asked if he'd observed any conflicts between Rosemary Joy and her classmates.

"Absolutely not," he said, "although a classroom teacher is not often privy to the social dynamics between students."

We discussed the case for a while longer. I explained Ralph's involvement in the case. Fallon seemed impressed that Ralph had gotten Brown to open up, but I assured him we were still stymied. We hadn't found any leads pointing to a likely suspect. I promised Fallon that we would keep him informed, and we left.

The week was ending, and we had not uncovered another clue that could lead us toward a more likely suspect and prove the innocence of Henry Brown. Ralph and I sat in my office and sipped coffee and went over the details and notes we'd accumulated. Agnes answered the phone when it rang and didn't interrupt us. Time went by, and I heard the outer door open and close. A young voice greeted Agnes. I glanced out the window and saw a green bike leaning against a lamppost.

"Excuse me, Ralph," I said. "I have to take care of something."

I opened the closet door and pulled out a new baseball and a bat, a Louisville Slugger model. Each object sported a bright red ribbon. I carried them into the outer office.

"Hi ya, Rusty?" I said. "A little birdie told me that today is a special day for you. Happy birthday. How does the world look through fourteen-year-old eyes?"

Rusty looked at what I carried, and a grin formed on his freck-led face.

"Wow! The world looks swell, Mr. Stone. Real swell! How did you know it was my birthday?"

"Hey, it's October fifteenth, isn't it? And didn't you know? I'm a detective, remember? Detectives know everything."

I handed him the gifts.

"These are from Miss Agnes and me," I said. "Happy birth-day, kiddo. I know baseball season is over, but I'll bet you've got a few more games to play before the weather turns."

"You bet I do! Thanks!"

He turned to Agnes.

"Thank you, too, Miss Agnes. What a great day!"

I reached into my pocket and pulled out a candy bar.

"This isn't much," I said, "but a fellow should have a sweet treat on his birthday, too."

I handed Rusty the candy bar, and he stuck in his pocket and grinned.

"Aren't you going to eat it?" Agnes said.

"You bet I am," Rusty said, "but I'll wait till I get home. Can-dy's pretty special. I'll share it with my folks."

What a kid, I thought. Rusty thanked us again and turned to leave, and Agnes called out.

"Oh, Rusty. Haven't you forgotten something?"

"I have?"

"Shouldn't you leave a newspaper?" she said.

Rusty rolled his eyes and pulled a copy of the afternoon edition from his bag. He handed it to her and touched his cap and left the office floating on a cloud. Agnes and I shared smiles, and I returned to my office.

Ralph and I loosened our ties and rolled up our sleeves and went back to work. I left instructions with Agnes to field telephone calls. So, I was surprised sometime later when she knocked on my door and opened it and told me that Lieutenant McCormick was on the line and wanted to speak to me. I reached for the phone.

"Yes, Mac."

"Something has come up. You'd better get over here."

It took us only a few moments to drive the few blocks to the police station. Mac was in his office behind his desk. Ralph and I each took a chair across from Mac.

"I've called you here because you've been investigating the Cleveland murder. We've been working under the assumption that the case was solved, and we had the murderer behind bars."

The assumption the case was closed? Ralph and I looked at each other. Where was Mac headed with this?

"I'm about to show you something that the press and the public know nothing about. We've kept this information in house for reasons you'll understand in a moment. But I need your word, both of you, that this goes no further. Do you understand?"

Mac looked at each of us in turn. We agreed. He reached into a desk drawer and pulled out two items, a dagger with an ivory handle and a small piece of paper with writing on it. He laid the items on the desk. The knife had a small triangle embossed on the handle. I was unable to read what was written on the paper.

"Go ahead, look at them," Mac said. "You can touch them. They've been dusted for prints."

Ralph picked up the dagger and studied it. I read the paper. It was a poem or part of a poem written in block print. I read it once and read it again. The words were familiar, but I couldn't come up with the title of the poem or its author on the spot.

"That is the weapon that was found next to the body of Rosemary Joy Cleveland," Mac said with a nod toward the dagger. "The poetry was found in the pocket of her pajamas."

"Odd place to find a poem," I said, "but not unusual for a student of literature. Maybe she was reading it or memorizing it in bed before she fell asleep."

Mac nodded.

"That's what we assumed," he said, "but when we checked for prints, we found none. She'd never touched it. We kept knowledge of these items in the station. Only a few of our personnel know about this. You probably wonder where this is headed. Did you read the papers this week, about the death of that young boy?"

"Yes, I read about it," I said. "It was out in the county. A couple of youngsters camping overnight near the river, I believe, on their farmland. Brothers, friends. Cousins, I think they were. One of them woke up to find his companion dead, murdered. The papers didn't say how the lad was killed. Don't tell me that death has a connection to the Cleveland case."

Mac reached into his desk and drew out two more items and placed them beside the dagger and the poem. The first item was another dagger with an ivory handle. It, too, had a triangle embossed on its handle, similar to the one on the first dagger but not identical. The other item was a piece of paper. I picked it up and read the passage, another poem written in block letter printing.

"The boy was stabbed in the abdomen. That wasn't reported in the papers. This dagger was the murder weapon," Mac said. "No prints were found on it. The poem was in the victim's pocket. No prints there either. His camping buddy, his cousin, has no idea how it got there or where the dagger came from either. He's pretty shook up as you can imagine. His cousin is murdered, but he's left untouched. He wakes up and discovers the body. It makes no sense. Look at both weapons carefully. Place them side by side."

I did. At first glance, they were a matched pair. Then, I noticed a difference between the two. The knife from the first stabbing, when held point down, showed an equilateral triangle on the handle with its point, its apex, pointed up. A horizontal line divided the triangle at its midsection. The next knife, when held point down, had a similar equilateral triangle on its handle, but this one lacked the horizontal line through its midsection. All other details such as size, weight, and material of the knives looked the same, as if they were a pair or came from a larger set of knives.

"What do you make of them?" Mac said, looking from me to Ralph and back to me.

"They must belong together, but I have no idea what the triangles signify," I said.

Ralph just shrugged.

"The M.O. for the murder of the boy is remarkably similar to that of the Cleveland woman," Mac said. "The knives, the poetry. How about the poetry? Do you recognize the poems?"

"The poems are vaguely familiar," I said. "I can't place them, but I'll see what I can find out."

I copied each poem into my book and made some notes and drawings of the knives.

"There's something else," Mac said. "I'm not sure if it means anything or not, but it's odd. The boys had stacked wood and kindling near their fire before they turned in for the night. The weather was warm enough that they didn't need much of a fire during the night, but they wanted to have wood on hand to cook breakfast in the morning. The wood they'd gathered was added to the fire sometime in the night, either before or after the murder. The killer must have stoked up the fire. Why would he do that?

What does that mean? Who does something like that? What kind of a mind does this guy have?"

"I can't answer that, but you know what this means. Whoever killed Miss Cleveland is still out there, Mac. You know it, and I know it. Henry Brown couldn't possibly be guilty, not in light of a similar stabbing death and this new evidence. Ralph and I will keep our mouths shut, but you can't sit on this. The press will find out. When it does, the citizens of our city will know what we in this room now know. Somewhere in Wichita, a serial killer is on the loose."

Your Involvement is Over
Your Involvement is Over

I needed time for reflection, and I found it with a drive in the country and then a shoeshine, to solve the riddle of the poetry. I could have gone to an expert like Dr. Fallon, of course, who would have recognized the poetry and given me titles and authors in moments, but I was sworn to secrecy and didn't want to arouse the professor's suspicions.

I was certain that the phrases left on the bodies were snippets of longer works, but I couldn't place them. I drove through the countryside with the top down on my roadster and recited the phrases out loud.

The paper found on Miss Cleveland read:

"Your half-tones delight me,

And I grow mad with gazing

At your blent colors."

The paper found on the young boy read:

"Nay, speak the truth, whatever it be,

Though it rend my bosom's core."

A drive in the country relaxed my mind and allowed me time to think without the distractions of a hectic world. Country roads and baseball. When I was faced with riddles and dilemmas, I turned to back roads and baseball for answers. Sometimes I found answers, sometimes I didn't, but a moment spent in either pursuit was a moment to treasure. I breathed the fresh air and admired the yellow countryside and the autumn trees and slowed to listen to the warble of a meadowlark on a fencepost. After a couple of hours in the country, I became certain that I'd read the poems in the past, but I was unable to recall the poets or titles of the works. I needed a shoeshine.

I drove back into town and headed for the Hotel Eaton on Douglas. Saturday morning traffic was light as was pedestrian traffic on the walks. I parked on the street and strolled through the lobby of the hotel. A lone patron puffed on a cigar and read the newspaper. He looked up when I went by and returned my nod and went back to his paper. The barber in his shop saw me through his window as I passed by. He had a customer in his chair, but he waved with his clippers, and I returned the wave. I found Ellis Waldo at his shoeshine station reading a worn copy of Walt Whitman's *Leaves of Grass*. Waldo lacked much formal education, but he didn't let that hold him back. He may have been the most well-read man I knew.

"Yes, sir, Mr. Stone," he said and laid the book aside. "Always a pleasure to see my favorite customer."

"Hah, I'd be curious to know how many favorite customers you have, Waldo."

He chuckled and wiped off the chair before I took a seat. He wiped my shoes clean and dipped his fingers into the polish and worked it into the leather.

"I don't know if you've spoken to Ralph, but he's been a tremendous help on a case I'm working on. I thought you might want to know," I said.

"He mentioned he was working with you, but he said he couldn't talk about it. He'd made a promise, he said."

Ralph had given his word to McCormick to remain silent, and his word was good.

"I see you're reading Walt Whitman."

"Yes, I am. I usually read prose. I like a good story, but I turn to poetry from time to time. Keeps my mind balanced, greases the wheels in my brain. Slows me down, too, and that's a good thing. Life's better lived at a slower speed, don't you think? You notice more, appreciate more. Music is sweeter, the girls are prettier, food tastes better when you slow down and take time to savor the flavors. That's what poetry does for me, anyway. It slows me down. Gives me pause."

"Well said. When I was a boy, my grandmother taught me to slow down. I'm not always a student of her advice, but she set a good example. She went slowly, always aware, noticed little things that others missed. Whitman sets a good example, too. I read some poetry recently, not by Whitman, that I've been turning over in my mind, just pieces of poems. I've been puzzling over their titles and who wrote them. Maybe you can help."

I recited the first phrase for Waldo. He mulled it over for a moment, and I recited the second phrase. He mulled that, too, and asked me to repeat the second poem again. I did.

"That one I recognize," he said. "'...speak the truth, whatever it be...' That comes from one of Bret Harte's poems, where he writes about Grant and the Civil War. The other one I don't recollect right off hand, but I believe it was written by a woman."

Waldo's comments triggered a memory. I thought I knew where I had seen the works. I thanked him. He went back to work shining my shoes, and we chatted about the recent World Series. He worked the leather to a shine and finished with his usual rag-popping flourish. I paid him and thanked him and shook his hand.

From the hotel, I drove to my place on Lewellen. Inside, I went straight to my bookshelf and reached for a familiar volume, an anthology of poetry. I lowered myself into an easy chair and opened the book to page ninety-two and began reading the poems listed under the name of Bret Harte. I lit a cigarette and read, and the clocks gonged the two o'clock hour. When I reached page ninety-five, I found the title I was looking for, "The Aged Stranger." The phrase in question, the words I copied from the paper found on the boy's body, made up the last two lines of the fifth verse, "Nay, speak the truth . . ." Good old Waldo. He was right. The poem belonged to Bret Harte.

I got up and poured a glass of cold tea from a pitcher in the refrigerator and returned to my chair. I spent the next hour or so thumbing through the anthology, reading works by female poets. When I reached the section on Amy Lowell, I read the poem at the top of page one hundred and ninety-one. Bingo, I said to myself. The poem was titled, "A Lady," and the phrase found on the body of Miss Cleveland made up the final lines of the first verse. I read it several times. ". . . half-tones delight me . . ." ". . . I grow mad with gazing . . ." ". . . blent colors." The words chilled me, not for their message but for the cold method in which they were delivered.

I closed my anthology and studied the title on its spine. It was a popular anthology, *Modern American Poetry and Modern British Poetry*, edited by Louis Untermeyer. My volume was a gift to me from my son, Dan. Untermeyer was a recognized scholar, and the book had received good reviews. Casual readers, such as myself, turned to poetry on a quiet evening at home. Of course, it was popular among academics, too. Many professors owned a copy—including an English professor at Wichita University, Dr. Wil Fallon. I'd seen Fallon's copy on his desk the day I met him, and I'd seen him clutching the volume as he left his office.

Was it merely a coincidence that Fallon owned Untermeyer's anthology? Was it also a coincidence that both of the notes found on the victims cited lines of poetry from the anthology? I didn't know the answers to those questions, but I didn't like coincidences. I faced a dilemma. I'd promised Lieutenant McCormick not to divulge details of the murders. I'd also promised Professor Fallon not to divulge his name and connection to the first victim unless my silence would obstruct the police investigation.

It was Saturday afternoon. I doubted I would catch McCormick at the station, but I tried to reach him. I made the call and was told that McCormick wasn't there, but he was expected to call in for messages. I left a message. I hung up the phone, and the clocks chimed four times. My stomach reminded me that I'd missed lunch. I thought about driving over to Tom's Inn, but I wanted to wait awhile in case Mac returned my call.

The contents of the kitchen didn't look promising, but I always kept eggs in the refrigerator and bread in the cupboard. I could cook eggs, and breakfast was a satisfying meal anytime of the day. Twenty minutes later, I sat down to a plate of scrambled eggs, buttered toast and fresh coffee. I reached for my fork, and the telephone rang. It was McCormick.

"What have you got for me, Stone?"

"Nice to hear your voice, too, Mac."

"Sorry," he said. "I didn't know you were so sensitive. Isn't it a beautiful day? I was so delighted that you'd called. Sorry I was out of my office. Is that better? Now, quit stalling and tell me what you've got for me."

"Your sarcasm stings. You always complain that I never give you anything," I said. "Well, I called to give you something. I've uncovered the source of the poems found on the victims, titles and poets."

"Yeah, we've got that, too," he said. "You're late as always."

"Don't tell me you have someone on the force who reads poetry."

"Are you kidding?" he said. "What we do have are cops who can dial a telephone. A call to the university was all it took. Some professor recognized the poems and the poets. We had the answers in a few minutes. Some detective, Stone. Like I say, you're late."

I wanted to ask which professor the police had spoken to, but I knew that asking that question would raise Mac's suspicions. I held my tongue.

"Where do you go from here?" I said. "You know Brown didn't commit the second murder. He was behind bars. And if you kept the details of the first murder in-house, the second murder wasn't a copycat killing. Only one person would own a pair of knives so similar in appearance. Only one person would leave snippets of poetry on the victims."

"Thanks for telling me what I already know," he said. "Sit on this, Stone. The police commissioner will make a statement to the press on Monday morning. Henry Brown will be released. Your involvement in the case is over. Your client will have no further involvement in this, either. He wanted Brown to be found innocent, didn't he? He'll get his wish. We'll take it from here."

What Mac said made sense. I hadn't found the killer, but that was not my job. Henry Brown was innocent, and he would be freed. Professor Fallon's suspicions were correct. It was up to the police to find the murderer. Mac and I said our goodbyes and hung up. I lit a cigarette and dialed another number. When Ralph Waldo answered, I repeated the details of my conversation with Lieutenant McCormick including his instructions to remain silent.

After we hung up, I crushed out my cigarette and stared at the food I'd prepared. The eggs had gone cold, as had the toast and coffee. I cleared the table and scraped the food off my plate and into the garbage can. I poured the coffee down the drain and reached for my car keys. The clocks chimed the five o'clock hour as I locked the door. I was headed for Tom's Inn for cold beer and a warm meal.

Lucille Wore a Blue Dress

The clock that Doc had found for me was perfect, a Chelsea Brass Marine on a mahogany base. It didn't look exactly like the clock it would replace, but that was fine. It was to be a gift from me. The brass trim on the replacement was shinier than that on the original, and its mahogany was darker, but I hadn't wanted a twin, just a close sibling. It would be a handsome addition to the mantel over Lucille Hamilton's fireplace. The first clock, the one that had been destroyed by a bullet, had belonged to Lucille's deceased husband. The replacement was a gift from me, similar in design and quality, but not an exact duplicate. Doc had called a few days earlier and told me it was ready, and now it sat on my table next to the radio. I had wrapped the gift in brown paper and tied the package with red ribbon and a bow.

The radio was tuned to KFH, and Uncle Ben Hammond, a cartoonist for the local newspaper, read the funnies to his audience. Hammond's voice greeted the city every Sunday morning. I chuckled at the antics of the Katzenjammer Kids and Little Orphan Annie and was both impressed and puzzled by Dick Tracy's gadgets. I couldn't imagine owning a wrist watch that also served as a two-way radio. Something that fantastic might help in fighting crime, but it would sure ruin a guy's life. What would it do to a day at the ballpark or a quiet drive in the country? I couldn't imagine people calling me anytime or anywhere. It would be like living in a telephone booth, and who would want that? I was pleased that the invention existed only in the mind of Chester Gould, Dick Tracy's creator, and would never exist anyplace but in the funny papers.

I read the Sunday news and sipped coffee and smoked cigarettes. My mind wasn't on the news. I thought about Professor Fallon and what I would say to him the next day. Henry Brown would be released, a good thing, but my investigation had done nothing to expose the murderer. Had the criminal remained in the background, there was a real possibility that Brown would have been tried and convicted and punished for a crime he didn't commit. Now that Brown was to be freed, the police would go after the real killer. That was not my job, as McCormick had made clear. I was no longer on the case. Still, it left an empty hole inside of me. I hated having to back away with the killer still on the loose, but I'd done what I was hired to do. All I could do now was report my findings to Fallon and bow out. I would not discuss anything with Fallon that was not made public by the police commissioner's statement to the press scheduled for Monday morning. I'd have to choose my words carefully.

Early that Sunday afternoon, I tucked the wrapped clock under my arm and walked down the steps to my roadster parked at the curb. Ghosts and goblins of the Halloween season had visited the neighborhood, and homes were decked out in orange and black. Paper cutout witches and goblins and skeletons hung from porch ceilings, and carved pumpkins grinned and scowled from steps and walks. I grinned, too. Halloween was always a favorite childhood celebration. I made a mental note to lay in a supply of sweet treats for my landlady to hand out to our neighborhood little ones. Our tacit agreement called for me to buy the candies. In exchange she would dole them out to the trick-or-treaters and bribe the tricksters from tossing eggs at our windows or my car.

I drove west and crossed the Little Arkansas River on Eleventh Street until it merged into Sim Park Drive. The drive ran along the banks of the Arkansas River in a southerly direction. I was headed for a white frame house on Clarence just south of First Street. My route wasn't the quickest or most direct to my destination, but it suited my mood to meander and gave me time to think.

The widow Lucille Hamilton had agreed to go on a date with me. This wasn't the first time we'd seen each other socially, but previously our time together had been limited to coffee or a bite to eat. On this day, she'd agreed to spend the afternoon with me.

I thought back to that first time we met. She had appeared at my office door, frightened and unsure but possessing a strong determination to find her husband. Her husband had gone missing, and she was going to find him, even if she didn't know how. The police had given her the brushoff, figuring her husband had gone on the lam like so many other husbands. She hired me to find him, and I did. His body showed up, floating face down in the river. The police ruled it a suicide, but Lucille didn't buy it. She was convinced he'd been murdered, and she convinced me, too. She hired me again, this time to find a killer the police said didn't exist. Over the following weeks, my investigation uncovered a scheme of betrayal that led to the murderer. It also led Lucille to distrust men, all men. Even though we'd developed an attraction toward one another, a crust of ice had formed over her heart, a crust of ice that needed time to thaw. She'd pushed me away. She needed to be alone, and I respected her wishes. Now, we would see each other again. Had the ice melted? I didn't know, but I was encouraged. Like I said, she'd agreed to spend a Sunday afternoon with me.

I reached Seneca and dropped south over the river to Douglas, then drove nine blocks west to Clarence. Broad, yellow leaves on catalpa trees blended with fiery red maples lining both sides of the street. The neighborhood was aflame with color. I parked my roadster on the brick street in front of the Hamilton home. The door opened on my first knock.

"Hello, Pete. Come in."

Lucille wore a blue dress with white polka dots and a broad white collar. Her blond hair was styled with pin curls just as it had been when we first met. She looked lovely, and I told her so. She smiled, and her eyes fell to the package under my arm.

"He comes bearing gifts. What's this about?"

"It's something that's long overdue. I hope you like it," I said.

The brown paper wrapping had come undone on one end, and the red ribbon had slipped and was falling loose. The package looked like it had lost a wrestling match with a six-year-old. Lucille stifled a laugh.

"Madam, I trust you'll forgive my gift's humble appearance and judge it solely on its contents," I said.

Lucille couldn't stifle her laugh any longer. She laughed out loud and nodded. I placed the package on a table, and she untied the ribbon. The paper fell away and revealed the clock. Her laughter stopped, and her hand went to her chest.

"Oh, dear. It's beautiful. It's so very beautiful." She threw her arms around my neck and hugged me. "Thank you for this. It's such a thoughtful gift. Would you please put it where it belongs?"

I carried the clock to the fireplace and set it atop the mantel.

"It's just perfect," she said.

She wiped a tear away with a handkerchief. She opened her arms, and we shared another hug. I held her in my arms, reluctant to let her go. She rested her head on my chest.

"I didn't realize how much I missed you," she said, "how much I've missed a man's arms around me."

She turned her face up to me and kissed me on the corner of my mouth. Her eyes glistened.

"I'm glad you're here. So, what are your plans for our after-noon together?" she said.

"Well, let's see, m'lady. I thought we might hop on a plane and wing our way to the gulf where we would set sail on a Carib-bean cruise."

She shook her head.

"I have nothing to wear."

"How about dining on escargot and veal in Gay Paree in the shadow of the Eiffel Tower?"

"Sorry, my French is rusty."

"A trip to the greatest city in the world. We'd catch a Broad-way play in the Big Apple."

"New York City is so crowded."

"To Rome for the opera? A stroll across London Bridge? Champagne and oysters in San Francisco?"

She shook her head and laughed.

"How about lunch downtown, and we'll see what develops from there?" she said.

"I'm crazy about you, kid," I said, and I was.

We ate at the Lassen Hotel. I drove with the top down on the roadster. I offered to button down the roof, but Lucille wouldn't hear of it. She wrapped a shawl around her shoulders and threw her head back and faced the sun and demanded it paint her cheeks pink.

We crossed over the river on Douglas, and at Market I turned north a block to First Street. Several cars were parked in front of the hotel, so I turned east on First Street and parked down the block. We strolled back to the hotel on the sidewalk. Lucille took my arm and admired the dresses and hats in a clothing store win-dow.

"This may not be my business," I said, "but how are you do-ing, Lucille. I mean financially?"

She squeezed my arm.

"I'm fine, Pete. Sidney had an insurance policy, and I'll be able to keep the house. I don't have money worries. I'll tell you, though, rattling around in that house by myself has grown tiresome. I'm ready to get out of the house more. I'd like to find some work, not only for the income but to be around people. The neighbors have been swell, and I have coffee with a couple of nice women, but I still get lonely. I did secretarial work before Sidney and I met. I've thought about going back to that, working in an office, but I'm open to most anything."

We crossed the street at the corner and entered the Lassen Hotel. A dozen years earlier, the owners of the hotel purchased a local radio station and changed its call letters to KFH—Kansas's Finest Hotel. The radio station gave the Lassen advertising and bragging rights, and it lived up to its billing. It was a fine hotel. We walked past the tobacco and newsstand and through its lobby furnished with plush sofas and chairs. A large chandelier hung from the high ceiling, and over a dozen other lamps were scattered throughout the room. A grand piano sat in a corner. Patrons in their Sunday finery chatted, smoked, and read newspapers and magazines. We went on to the dining room and were seated at a table for two near a window, and the waitress took our order.

"So, can you tell me about your current case," Lucille said, "or is it hush-hush?"

That was a question I had hoped to avoid. I met Lucille when she needed a detective's help, and I had obliged. By the time I had solved the case, she'd witnessed gunplay, violence, and death, some of it right in her living room. Afterwards, she made it clear that she was not a fan of my chosen profession.

"I'm working on a case, but I'll close it tomorrow after I visit with my client. It wasn't difficult work, and I was never in danger. You know, a detective spends most of his time looking for clues or sitting on a stakeout, waiting and watching, sometimes for hours at a time. Those hours alone give a guy time to pause and ponder and wonder why he ever got into this line of work. Most of the time it's the most boring job in the world."

"Except when it isn't the most boring job in the world," she said. "Then things move fast. Sometimes there's violence. Sometimes there's death."

I nodded.

"True. Sometimes there's chaos, mayhem, and a detective has to think fast and move fast. There are moments of danger. My current case didn't put me in danger. My client hired me to prove that another man was innocent of a crime—murder. It turns out my client was correct. The suspect was innocent and will be released tomorrow, although what I did proved little to help his case. Nevertheless, my client and the accused man will both be satisfied, and by tomorrow afternoon I'll be out of work again. That's the way it goes. I should mention that along with hours of boredom, being a detective is a sure way to dodge those pesky lines on payday. I never know when or if payday will arrive. Nothing is certain in this business. That's part of its charm. It's the uncertainty that keeps me on my toes, keeps my heart pumping."

She reached across the table and squeezed my hand.

"Thanks for not trying to sugarcoat it," she said. "You'd crack under the strain if you worked an eight-to-five job. If you were in the circus, you'd be an acrobat on the high wire."

"Funny you should mention the circus," I said and pulled a pair of tickets out of my jacket pocket. "You must be psychic. Since you declined my offer of a Caribbean cruise, I've chosen to take you to the circus this afternoon."

Lucille laughed.

"Wonderful," she said.

Our meals arrived, and we enjoyed our food with no further discussion of my line of work. Instead, we chatted about possible work positions for Lucille as we dined on tenderloin and asparagus tips. The dining room was busy, but patrons spoke in hushed tones. A pianist in the lobby played pieces by Chopin. The waitress cleared the table and served chocolate mousse for dessert. We finished with coffee and cigarettes.

"I know I'm repeating myself," Lucille said, "but this is wonderful. May I ask if you often dine like this?"

"Kiddo, I'm a burgers and beans man," I said and grinned. "However, I do enjoy dining with a woman who deserves to be treated like a lady."

"Does a lady attend the circus?" she said.

"She does today," I said.

I settled the tab, and we left the hotel. The Tom Mix Circus was performing in Wichita, and they had pitched their tent in a pasture west of the river between Thirteenth and Twenty-First Streets. I parked the roadster near other cars, and we walked along with a crowd moving toward the Big Top. Up ahead we heard a commotion and watched people running. A Klaxon horn sounded, and its loud ahooga alerted the crowd to part for the arrival of Tom Mix, who sat behind the wheel of his luxury automobile, a Cord 812 Phaeton. Tom Mix exited the vehicle wearing western garb, and an assistant arrived leading Tony the Wonder Horse. Mix took the reins and leapt into the saddle, and Tony reared up on his hind legs. Mix removed his ten gallon hat and swung it over his head and waved it at the crowd. Everyone cheered and whistled and applauded. Tom Mix and Tony disappeared into a smaller tent while the crowd filed into the Big Top.

"I'll take this over New York or Paris, anytime," Lucille said.

"I knew you were a lady," I said.

We munched on popcorn and enjoyed the show, the acrobats and gymnasts and clowns and elephants and all the rest. Along with their usual cast of performers, the circus showcased special talent as well. Emmett Kelly, the nationally known clown from Sedan, Kansas, had returned to his home state to perform as Weary Willie, the sad-faced hobo clown with a broom, who swept up the circus ring following the performances. He even tried to sweep up the spotlight that moved across the ground while the crowd laughed and applauded. Each time he exited, the crowd favored him with a standing ovation. Also on hand were McKenzie Midget Autos, built by Wichita's Leo McKenzie. With clowns at the wheels, the tiny cars wove around the center ring and narrowly avoided colliding with each other as the crowd hooted and hollered. Tom Mix returned to the center ring and led Tony the Wonder Horse through a series of intricate tricks that delighted everyone. Lucille squeezed my hand and laughed throughout the afternoon, and I savored the joy that danced in her eyes.

Later that day, after the circus was over, I held Lucille in my arms, and we watched the sun settle on the horizon. The temperature had cooled, and a flame flickered in Lucille's fireplace. We stood in her living room and watched the sky through her picture window, then we sat down on her sofa and gazed into the fire. We sipped on coffee and brandy.

"It's been too long since I've enjoyed a day like this," she said. "Thank you."

"No need to thank me," I said. "The feeling is mutual. I needed this day as much as you did."

Lucille rested her head on my chest, and I kissed the top of her head.

"What does this mean, Pete?"

"It means we enjoy each other's company, and we had a good day together," I said. "It also means we should enjoy each other's company again. We'd be foolish not to. Let's don't be foolish."

"Okay, let's don't be foolish. Promise me you won't rush me though. Can you do that?"

"Promise," I said.

We finished our drinks and hugged and kissed goodbye, and I drove the roadster back to my place on Lewellen.

♦ ♦ ♦

I Met Him in the Philippines

I Met Him in the Philippines

I arrived at the Liberal Arts Building a bit earlier than my scheduled appointment time with Professor Fallon. The police commissioner had made his announcement on the radio, and I drove to the campus as soon as the report was finished. Agnes and I listened to it on the Zenith radio in my office, and I saw no reason to delay meeting with Fallon. He was in class when I arrived, but he would be in his office soon. My friend, history professor Ethan Alexander, was also out of his office, so I loitered in the hallway outside the door of Room 205. I heard voices, chatter and laughter, coming from a room down the hall, so I drifted in that direction and eyed a pair of students through an open doorway.

"Hello. Mr. Stone, isn't it? Come on in," said a feminine voice. I recognized its owner as Cynthia Buckman, the graduate student I'd met in Fallon's office. "What brings you to our humble abode, aka slave quarters?"

Cynthia was in a small office crammed with desks and chairs. Arthur Cross, her fellow graduate assistant, sat at the desk next to hers.

"Hello, Cynthia, Arthur," I said. "I was down the hall and heard voices and decided to snoop. Occupational hazard, I guess. Don't let me interrupt. I'm just waiting for Professor Fallon to return to his office."

"Swell. Pull up a chair and take a break," Cynthia said. "That's what we're doing. This is our brief mid-morning revolt against the tedium of research, teaching, and more research."

Arthur hadn't spoken yet, but he acknowledged my presence with a polite nod.

"Are you sure you wouldn't rather be alone?" I said.

Cynthia glanced at Arthur and back at me and laughed.

"Alone? Arthur and me? No, no, no. There's nothing like that going on here. Arthur and I have been assigned to work together, but you'll find no romance in this office. Alas, poor Yorick pines for another, an unrequited love, I'm afraid. Arthur's starry eyes take little notice of the fair Cynthia at his elbow, whose heart flutters like a bird in her breast each time he deigns to glance her way."

Cynthia giggled, and Arthur turned red.

"Cynthia, please," he said.

I had to smile. The young lady was having good-natured fun at her classmate's expense, but her teasing wasn't cruel. Cynthia was a slender young woman with straight, brown hair that could have used a brushing, and the dress she wore was a bit rumpled, but her wit and humor were contagious. She gazed at the world through a pair of round spectacles. Arthur appeared to be sullen and dour, but that could have been a reaction to Cynthia's teasing. His hair was trimmed short, and his pudgy frame suggested too much time spent in the library and too little time exercising.

"Tell me about your research," I said.

I directed the question to both of them, but Cynthia answered.

"Well, there's my research, and there's Arthur's research, and then there's Dr. Fallon's research," she said. "Doing my own research is fine, and I hope to finish my thesis this semester, maybe next. Same with dear Arthur here. If that's all we had to do, we'd be cruising down easy street. However, we also have to teach composition classes to students who hate to write and find any

132

excuse to avoid their assignments, and we assist Dr. Fallon in his research. He has to publish his own work, too, you know. It's a heavy load. Hence the 'slave' moniker."

"Is your professor a harsh taskmaster?" I said.

"No, he's a good guy, really. It's just the way the system is here or any other university I suppose. Dr. Fallon has to publish if he wants to keep his job, and we have to help him do research if we want to keep ours. That's not unusual. It's the same in every department. No one is picking on us. For our efforts our tuition is paid, our books are purchased, and we make enough extra to dine on all the ketchup soup and stale bread we can eat."

Her laughter told me that the soup and bread remark was an exaggeration, but I knew from experience that a graduate student had to work hard to make ends meet. My son, Dan, didn't complain when he was a student, but I knew he went through some rough patches, too.

Another pair of students, two males, entered the room chatting together. They paused their conversation when they noticed me and dropped their books on their respective desks. Cynthia caught their puzzled expressions and introduced me.

"Mr. Stone is doing nonacademic research for Dr. Fallon," she said.

I was impressed that she recalled the words Fallon used when he introduced me to Arthur and herself. She introduced the pair as Tony Hathaway who worked for Dr. Alexander, my friend the history professor, and Howie Solomon who worked with Dr. Landis, another English professor. I shook hands with each of them.

"I know Ethan Alexander and admire him," I said to Tony, "but I haven't met Dr. Landis."

Howie Solomon looked perturbed.

"I haven't been with Dr. Landis for very long," he said.

An awkward silence fell over the room.

"Howie worked with Dr. Fallon during the spring semester," Cynthia said, "but they had a falling out."

I wondered about the nature of their falling out but sensed it was an internal matter they didn't want to discuss further. I glanced at my watch.

"I'd better go," I said. "Thanks for the visit."

The men gave me a wave, and Cynthia touched my arm.

"Hey, nothing to Dr. Fallon about our chat, okay?" she said. "He really is a good guy, but he might take it the wrong way. I don't want him to think that we're complaining."

"Mum's the word," I said and left the office.

Students moved down the hallway toward their next classes. A bulletin board was decked out in black and orange. A notice in the center of the board read, "Faculty/Student Halloween Party," and gave details as to the time and place. It was to be held in the Commons Building on Saturday evening, October 30th. All students and faculty were urged to attend, and prizes would be given for best costumes. Special consideration would go to those dressed as literary characters.

The door to Room 205 was ajar, and I heard voices inside, one of which belonged to Fallon and the other to an unknown male. The tones of their voices suggested they were talking colleague to colleague and mildly disagreed with one another. Since I had an appointment, I knocked and entered on Fallon's invitation. He sat behind his desk, this time covered with several stacks of student papers. The familiar copy of Untermeyer's anthology rested on its usual corner of the desk. Seated across from him was another man I didn't know.

"Excuse me," I said. "I don't mean to interrupt. Should we reschedule?"

"No, no, come in," Fallon said. "My esteemed colleague, Dr. Sherman Landis, and I were just debating the merits, if any, of replacing *Huck Finn* in our American novel curriculum with Sinclair Lewis's *Babbitt*. Sherman, this is Mr. Pete Stone."

Fallon gave my name with no title or mention of what I did for a living. It seemed to matter little to Dr. Landis, Howie Solomon's mentor. I recalled the first time I'd visited Fallon in his office and how he'd been concerned that someone might see him talking to me and learn that I was a detective. That concern no longer seemed to exist. Landis offered a perfunctory how-do-you-do and a limp handshake from his seated position then turned his attention back toward Fallon. Fallon gestured at an empty chair, and I took a seat.

"Here's what I think," Landis said, and when he was sure he had recaptured Fallon's attention he proceeded to hold forth on how today's modern student would better relate to Lewis's character, Babbitt, than Twain's outdated Huckleberry Finn, as if relating to the novel's protagonist was the primary purpose of study and analysis. Fallon listened with pursed lips. I listened to the men with one ear and glanced at the title of a manuscript on the desk, "Shakespeare and the Four Humors." Its author was Dr. Wilfred Fallon. Landis finished speaking, and Fallon looked down and shook his head. The he looked at me with a devilish grin.

"Let's ask Mr. Stone what he thinks," Fallon said.

Dr. Landis glanced at me and turned back to Fallon with an expression that suggested, why should anyone care what this guy thinks?

"How about it, Mr. Stone?" Fallon said. "Should we continue teaching the 'outdated' classic, *Huck Finn*, or should we adopt a more modern approach and replace it with the contemporary *Babbitt*? Are you familiar with the novels?"

I assured the pair that I had read both of them.

"It's difficult for me to make a choice because they are so unlike one another," I said. "I've enjoyed reading each of them, and they are both important, in my opinion. However, I'm a huge fan of Mark Twain, and although I admire Sinclair Lewis, I've returned to Mark Twain a number of times. I think a student of literature who has not read and studied *Huck Finn* should consider himself uneducated."

Landis mumbled something under his breath and rose from his chair and left the room. Fallon chuckled.

"He's really a good teacher," he said. "He's a bit full of himself, and he opines often, but he cares about the education of our students. I think he's a bit jealous that I was selected to chair the department instead of him. Not to worry. A little disagreement between colleagues is good from time to time."

I nodded.

"Incidentally, I was in the graduate assistants' office earlier, and I met Landis's assistant, Howie Solomon. Solomon and Miss Buckman mentioned that he'd once worked for you, but you parted ways. Under normal circumstances, I wouldn't be interested in office squabbles, but these aren't normal circumstances. Maybe you should tell me what happened."

Fallon drummed his fingers on his desk.

"Howard Solomon. It was an unfortunate incident," he said, "but we've put it behind us. I had gone over some of his work, his personal research, and I noted several instances of plagiarism, work taken without acknowledgement or citation from minor authors and from little known articles. A casual reader might not have caught the discrepancies, but as his advisor I was not a casual reader. I was familiar with his sources, and I pointed out his plagiarism. He denied having stolen the work. When I produced the original articles and pointed out his cheating, he grew defensive and claimed it was merely an oversight and not important. I was livid at his cavalier attitude to a serious offense and recommended he be censured or even expelled from the program altogether. He pleaded his case to the dean who took pity on him and allowed him to remain at the university if he cleaned up his research and promised to demonstrate more care in the future. I refused to continue as his advisor, so he now works with Landis. This is the first time I've discussed the situation since it occurred. I assumed he dropped it and moved on."

"He's still majoring in English," I said. "How can he continue in the program without taking your classes or having contact with you?"

"He's already completed his requirements with me. He's nearing completion of his program. We may have an awkward moment or two this semester, but he'll be allowed to complete his degree. Frankly, if he does show remorse for his actions and continues working in a scholarly fashion, I will wish him well with no hard feelings."

I turned to the purpose for our appointment.

"There was an announcement on the radio this morning," I said. "The police commissioner spoke. You may have been in the classroom when it aired. Did you hear it?"

"No, no, I didn't. Is it good news?"

"I think you'll be pleased," I said.

I gave Fallon a summary of the radio report without divulging more information than had been made public. The commissioner spoke about the knives appearing to be similar to each other and perhaps belonging to a matched set, but he didn't mention the actual markings on the knives. He also said nothing about the snippets of poetry found on the victims' bodies. Those were details that McCormick had shared with me but remained unknown to the public.

"So you see, the police now have two murders to solve," I said, "and the modus operandi, the method used to commit each separate crime, is very similar, too similar in each case. The murders were committed by one person. It's impossible that the murders were committed by two different killers. Since Henry Brown was behind bars when the second victim was murdered, he couldn't have committed that crime. And since the second murder was so alike in detail to the first, Brown couldn't have committed the first one either. Henry Brown is innocent, just as you suspected. He'll be freed today. In fact, he's probably already on the street."

Fallon's reaction, which was no reaction at all, took me by surprise. He looked at me as if I weren't in the room, as if he didn't see me. His eyes were on my face, but I sensed if I stuck out my tongue and went cross-eyed, he wouldn't notice. He said nothing when I told him Brown was now a free man.

"Professor? Did you hear me? Henry Brown is free. Isn't that what you wanted?"

Fallon came back to the present.

"Yes, yes, it is. Forgive me. Well done. Brown is free. That's wonderful, but a murderer continues to roam our streets."

"Yes, that's true, but the police will find him."

"I read about the second victim in the newspaper," he said. "Just a boy. How cruel."

"Murder is a cruel business," I said.

I placed a check on the desk.

"What's this?" he said.

"A refund. Your retainer more than covered my expenses. And thanks for the 'well done,' but I don't deserve it. If the murderer hadn't committed the second crime, the cops would still have Brown behind bars."

Fallon stared at the check in his hand, then leaned over the desk and placed it in front of me.

"I'd like you to keep this, Mr. Stone. I'd like you to remain in my employ, if you would be so kind. Continue your investigation. I want you to find this killer."

"Wait a minute, professor. I didn't bargain for this. You asked me to find proof that Brown was innocent. I can't just take over this case. This is police business now. Working to get Brown free was one thing. The police had given up on the case. They thought they had their murderer. Things have changed now. They'll have their detectives investigating. They won't welcome a private investigator muddying the water. What's your interest in this, anyway? I thought you only wanted to see Brown set free."

"I did want Brown free, and I'm grateful. I believed in his innocence."

"And he is innocent. So, what else is there?"

Fallon went silent. I stared at him, and he struggled to meet my gaze. Suddenly, it hit me.

"The second victim, the boy," I said. "Don't tell me you knew him? You knew him? The young boy?"

Fallon fidgeted.

"Yes, I knew him, at least I know his family. Years ago, I knew his grandfather," he said.

Dr. Wilfred Fallon was full of surprises—and coincidences.

"Wait a minute," I said. "First, you hire me to prove the innocence of Henry Brown, who it turns out is not only your son who you've never met but the brother of victim number one, Rosemary Joy Cleveland, your former student. And now you tell me that you knew the second victim, a young boy, as well as his family and grandfather. Those are strong coincidences, professor. Or are they coincidences? There's more. What else aren't you telling me?"

"I thought we covered everything when you came to my home," he said. "I didn't expect this. You can't believe I knew this killing would continue. I told you about my private affairs. I divulged more to you about myself and my personal life than I have to anyone else."

"Coincidences, professor. The police don't like coincidences," I said. "Neither do private cops."

"I can appreciate that," he said. "I don't understand what's happening any more than you do. That's why I want you to continue to work for me. It isn't necessary to muddy the waters, as you say. Go to the police. Work with them. I'm certain you have allies on the force. Work with them on my behalf. Do what you have to do. Say what you have to say. Find that killer."

"Are you giving me permission to use your name with the police? They're going to want know why I'm involved."

"Do what you have to do. I only care about finding the murderer."

I pondered his words.

"Okay," I said. "Tell me the rest of it. Tell me about the boy and the grandfather."

Fallon leaned back and gathered his thoughts.

"Red Gulliver. I met him in the Philippines. I enlisted in the army, the 20th Kansas Volunteer infantry, when I was a young man. This was just before the turn of the century, of course. You would have been a small boy. I thought I was answering Governor Leedy's call to fight in Cuba, but my unit was sent to the Philippines to quell an insurrection in Manila. That's where I met Red Gulliver, another dumb Kansas kid like myself, full of bluster and beans and looking for adventure. We fell in together and became fast friends.

"We saw some fighting, and we lost a lot of men, not only to fighting but to tropical diseases. Red contracted cholera and died over there. I was with him at the end. He gave me a few personal effects to pass on to his girlfriend back home. Said he trusted me more than military officials to see that she got them, and he wanted me to talk to her, to let her know that his last thoughts were of her.

"When I got back to the states, I looked her up. He'd left his girlfriend in Mt. Hope, but she was no longer there. I found her in Wichita, in a home for unwed mothers. Seems that Red had already left her with his legacy, the beginnings of a baby girl."

"Don't tell me," I said. "You took them under your wing."

"Red was my pal," Fallon said. "What could I do? He died too young. He never got to know his daughter. For that matter, he never got to know Jean Harlow, either. What a waste. I couldn't just ignore his family. I helped when I could, a few bucks, some groceries now and then. His girlfriend found work as a clerk in a store and raised the daughter on her own. She never married. She died not long ago, old before her time. The daughter did marry, but she and her husband have struggled as farmers. I've helped them a time or two, but they've never faced anything like this. They had two children, a boy and a girl. Now, they have only one child remaining, just their daughter. How does any parent handle the death of a child, especially one who is murdered?"

I took a breath and strummed my fingers on the arm of my chair.

"If I go to the police," I said, "the first thing they'll want to know is the name of my client and why my client has hired me. If I tell them who you are and reveal your connections to the victims, they're going to want to talk to you. They may even try to arrest you as a suspect. Like I said, the police don't like coincidences."

It was Fallon's turn to take a breath.

"Do what you have to do. Find the killer. Bring him to justice."

I'm a Bad Penny

I'm a Bad Penny

"This is police business, Stone. I thought you understood that. I'm busy. I don't have the time or the inclination to bang gums with a two-bit keyhole peeper when we have a killer loose in the city. Get out of my office. Ease right back out the door and close it softly. Slam it shut if it gives you any satisfaction. Just make sure that when the door is closed, you're on the other side of it."

"You know, Mac, your attitude could put a damper on our long-standing friendship and mutual respect for one another. A guy with thinner skin might be hurt by your words, might think you actually mean the terrible things you say. 'Two-bit keyhole peeper?' That's not true, and you know it. I've rarely peeped a keyhole and never for a lousy two-bits. I have my standards."

Mac groaned and shook his head.

"Listen," I said. "I'm involved in this, like it or not. I'm a bad penny. I always show up. I'm the gum on the bottom of your shoe. I'm not going away. I have a client, and my client wants results. He wants these murders solved. He knows this is police business, but he also knows I've been conducting my own investigation, or at least I was until Henry Brown was released. I'm willing to help the police. I'll give you what I have, but only if you work with me. We can work together or bump heads with each other. Either way, you're stuck with me."

"Help the police, huh? You'll give us only what you want us to have. You'll feed us with an eyedropper, that's what you'll do."

I said nothing. The police had staked their chips on Henry Brown being the murderer, and that hadn't panned out. Their hand had gone bust. Now they needed all the help they could get. Mac knew it, and I knew it. He rose from his desk and hovered over me as I sat in the chair. He whispered something intended for his ears only. He crossed the room and closed the door to his office. He returned to his desk and sat down.

"What have you got?" he said. "What's your interest in this? Who's your client?"

I held up my hand.

"In due time. You first," I said. "I'll answer your questions, but you give first."

"Alright. You said it. You were conducting an investigation," Mac said. "We thought we'd investigated the murder. We thought we had the killer behind bars."

"I've seen the knives and the notes left on the victims. Let's look at the files."

McCormick shook his head, but he lifted the receiver on his phone and punched a button and spoke. A few minutes later, there was a knock on the door, and my pal, Marjorie Mattox, came in carrying a pair of files. She nodded at me, and I returned the nod. She handed the files to Mac. He thanked her, and she left the room.

Mac handed me the written report from Rosemary Joy Cleveland's file. I scanned it but saw nothing we hadn't gone over before. I looked over the inventory of items found in her room and saw nothing new there either. I noted the absence of a diary that her friend in Emporia, Ida Mae Parsons, said she kept.

"Nothing we haven't gone over," I said and handed back the paperwork. "How about photographs? I haven't seen any pictures of the scene."

Mac handed me several photos. The first shots were of the room itself looking much as I remembered it. The only difference was that Rosemary Joy's personal effects were visible in the photos. They hadn't been removed yet, as they had been when I visited the boardinghouse. Her bed was unmade. Sheets and a blanket lay rumpled at the foot of the bed. A book lay open on the table. Another photo identified it as her Bible.

I shuffled those photos to the bottom of the pile and looked at the next one and drew in my breath. It showed the body lying on the floor, atop the area rug that Miss Edna had mentioned to me on my visit. The rug was stained with a pool of blood. The knife had been removed from the victim by Henry Brown, so the photograph showed only a dark stain on her chest. Another shot from a more remote angle showed the body lying beneath the ceiling fan. The blades were blurred in the photo indicating that the fan was running at the time. A close up shot showed the victim's face, and she looked remarkably at peace. Another shot taken a step back showed the upper half of her body. Her left arm was extended, as were the fingers on her left hand, but her right arm was bent at the elbow, and her right hand was drawn into a fist.

"Let me see your magnifying glass," I said.

"What do you see?" he said.

He opened a drawer and withdrew his magnifying glass. I held it over the photo of the victim's fist. She appeared to be clutching something, but only a tiny piece of the object was visible, and it was too small to identify.

"What does this look like to you?" I said and passed the picture and glass across the desk.

"I can't tell. It's not clear. Is it a chain, the end of a chain? A bracelet, maybe?" he said.

I rechecked the inventory of personal effects.

"No jewelry listed here," I said. "Why not ask Sergeant Holliday? See if he recalls seeing any jewelry."

Mac pushed a button and spoke into his phone again, and Holliday appeared a few moments later. Mac handed Holliday the photograph and the magnifying glass. He scanned the photo then read the inventory list. He shook his head.

"Nah, I don't recall anything like jewelry," he said. "She was in her nightclothes. Don't women take off their jewelry when they go to bed? She didn't have a jewelry box, at least one that I saw. I checked everything in."

"Are her effects still in the property room?" I said.

The sergeant shook his head.

"Nope. Brown collected her effects when he was released," he said. "There was no one else to claim them."

Mac nodded, and Holliday left the room.

"It's probably nothing," he said, but neither of us was willing to overlook a niggling little detail. He reached for the phone and gave instructions to Marjorie Mattox in the outer office.

"Let's move on to the murder of the boy," he said.

I read through the file on the boy. His name was Andrew Egan, and he had been on an overnight camping trip with his cousin, Walter Egan. Walter's dad had given his son a pup tent for his birthday, and the boys were eager to try it out. It was a school night, so they hadn't gone far from home, just down to the river that ran through their land. They farmed in Sedgwick County northwest of Wichita.

There was a knock at the door, and Marjorie Mattox entered the room.

"I spoke to the coroner's office," she said. "Their notes say that a necklace was removed from Cleveland's right fist. No description of the necklace itself. Marks on the victim indicate she may have pulled it from her neck either during the struggle with the killer or immediately after receiving her stab wound. The necklace was sent to the property room."

Mac thanked her, and she left.

"Someone probably received it in the property room and put it with her other effects but failed to note it on the inventory list," he said.

I nodded agreement, and we turned our attention back to the Egan file.

"This just doesn't make sense," Mac said, and I agreed. "One boy killed, the other left alone. Why? What's the motive behind this? What if the other boy, the cousin, had woken up during the stabbing?"

"You know what would have happened," I said. "Both boys would have been killed. As horrible as it is, the cousin is fortunate he's a heavy sleeper."

I looked at the photographs. First, a young woman, now a young boy. These pictures would haunt me in the still of the night. As reported, the boy had been pierced in the abdomen. The knife was visible in the photos.

"What do you make of the fire?" I said. "Why would the killer stoke up a fire?"

"I have no idea," Mac said. "It was dark? He wanted more light to see what he was doing?"

I didn't like that explanation, and I could tell that Mac didn't either.

"No, no, he'd have been carrying a flashlight," I said. "He needed light to walk the trail, to get to their campsite, and to identify his victim. This killing wasn't random. He chose Andrew Egan for a reason. The fire is significant for another reason, but I don't know what that reason is. The killer is telling us something."

There was a knock at the door, and Marjorie came in with coffee.

"You boys look like you need refreshment," she said.

Mac and I thanked her, and she left. Mac lit a cigar, and I lit a cigarette.

"Alright, Stone. It's your turn," he said. "What's your interest in this? Who are you working for?"

I'd been dreading this conversation, but I'd been expecting it. It was why I insisted upon learning what the police had before I revealed my client's name. Fallon had given me permission to say anything necessary to become involved in the investigation, even though I'd warned him about what to expect. I considered the clues the police and I had uncovered, and the only common element I could find between them was Professor Fallon himself. There were too many coincidences to suspect anyone else of the crimes. I didn't think Fallon was guilty, but what I thought wouldn't matter, not to McCormick. Mac hadn't spent time with Fallon as I had. He didn't know him. Maybe I didn't know Fallon, either. Mac would draw the same conclusion I did. He would suspect Fallon of the murders. If I revealed his name, I would unleash a shower of bricks upon myself.

"My client is a professor here in town, at Wichita University," I said, "and before you jump to conclusions, I spoke to my client this morning in his office. He wants this killer caught, just as you and I do. He's given me permission to talk to you—in exchange for the information you've just given me. I'm telling you this, Mac, because I want you to understand that my client wants the murders solved. That's his only interest. He wants justice. He wants justice whether it comes from the police or from me."

I stopped talking and watched McCormick. He puffed on his cigar and waited. I knew that the best way to learn what another person is thinking is to shut my yap and wait, to listen to what he says. The problem was that McCormick knew this as well as I did. McCormick was the greatest listener I had ever known. He could persuade the Sphinx to spill its guts. The clock ticked. A knock on the door broke the silence.

"Not now!" he barked, and the sound of footsteps retreated down the hallway. "This professor have a name?" he said.

I nodded and divulged his name. Mac remained calm. I was leery. Anyone who'd experienced Kansas weather knew that the skies grew calm just before the tornado hit.

"So, why all the interest?" he said.

I told Mac about Fallon and his position at the university, about Fallon's relationship with Miss Cleveland, about his admiration for her as his student. I told him that Fallon knew about the relationship between Cleveland and Brown, but I did not mention that Fallon was Brown's father. I saw no reason to divulge that. I also explained that Fallon had met and befriended Egan's grandfather while serving in the Philippines. I didn't mention that Fallon had gifted money to the victims or their families over the years. Mac listened and puffed on his cigar and sipped coffee and listened some more. His eyes never left mine. When I stopped talking, he stared at me for a solid minute. It may have been an hour. Finally, he spoke.

"Just how long have you been withholding this information?" he said.

"I haven't been withholding information," I said. "I already told you about my client's interest in proving Brown's innocence. I learned about my client's interest in the boy a few hours ago. That's why I'm here. I'm following my client's wishes. I was as surprised to learn this information as you are."

I was also surprised that Mac had remained calm. I suspected that inside he was seething.

"The poetry found on the victims," he said. "I told you about the poetry several days ago. Did it occur to you to connect the dots, to trace those clues to an English professor? Poetry and an English professor? Do those two elements sound like they might go together? Does that trigger anything in your pea-sized brain, Stone?"

"Fallon knows you'll want to talk to him. He has nothing to hide. Go ahead. Talk to him."

McCormick said nothing. He stared at me and shook his head. "What?" I said.

He mumbled something to himself. He may have been counting to ten.

"What else is there? What else are you not telling me? You have more. I'm trying to imagine what that is, but you're through talking, aren't you? Get out of here, or do I have to show you the door? I doubt you could find the door on your own. I doubt you could find a drop of water in a rainstorm. Get out."

I rose from my chair and walked across the room. Somehow, I found the door on my own. I opened it and left.

A Copse of Cottonwood Trees

S ome of the richest, darkest farmland in Kansas could be found in Sedgwick County. Farmers struggled to make a living there, just as they did further west on the prairie, but most folks survived, subsisting on a few acres given over to winter wheat, or corn, or milo. A family garden often thrived near the house, and a few head of livestock grazed in the pasture. Maybe the farmer made enough so the youngsters got new pairs of shoes in the fall. Maybe they wore the hand-me-downs an older brother or sister wore the year before. Sewing day followed laundry day, and mother stitched what needed stitching and patched what needed patching, anything to spare the garment from the rag bag. Neighbors struggled side by side. Few complained. Who would listen if they did?

A cool front blew in from the north on Tuesday morning with a promise of rain later in the day, so I drove the roadster with the top buttoned up and rolled over gravel roads toward Mt. Hope. Before I left Wichita, I called Ralph Waldo and asked him to talk to Henry Brown. I wanted details on the necklace his sister wore. It was probably nothing, a minor detail, but when you have little to go on, little details matter.

When I saw a farmer, I tooted my horn and waved and always received a friendly wave in return. Many I recognized from my days of picking up eggs, milk, and produce in the country and delivering the products to stores and restaurants and homes in the city. Those days before the Depression changed my life along with the lives of so many others.

I had a partner back then, before I became a private eye, and we shared a business—a panel truck and a list of sellers and buyers. We got by, but when the economy collapsed, we realized our small business wouldn't support two families. We talked it over and decided to flip a coin, winner take all. I lost the toss, and my partner became sole owner of the business—the truck and the list of customers. He took it worse than I did. I slapped him on the shoulder and told him he won the business fair and square. I shook his hand and wished him the best, and I meant it. I didn't look back.

I turned north toward Mt. Hope, and when the road jogged at the correction line, I slowed down and eyeballed the Nicklaus homestead and noticed that the buildings, the house, the barn and the shed looked more weathered and rundown than I remembered. I didn't see anyone outside. Sometimes just keeping up day to day, just staying even became too much and overwhelmed the best of us. Sometimes life seemed too impossible to bear. Buildings declined along with their owners, and when they did, they almost never came back. They just bent over and leaned closer to the ground and finally collapsed, buildings and people alike.

I drove into Mt. Hope and idled at the downtown intersection, a bank on one corner, a hotel, a grocery store, and a community building on the others. Farmers in overalls and wives in threadbare dresses, some carrying a baby or holding a toddler's hand, strolled the walks. Older youngsters were in the schoolhouse on the west edge of town.

I continued through town and on into the country. There was little activity in the fields. Farmers had finished drilling their winter wheat and worked on equipment in sheds closer to the houses. A few miles north of town, I crossed a bridge over the Arkansas River. When I reached the next intersection, I turned east and in a quarter of a mile came to a mailbox marked Egan. A meadowlark perched on a fencepost across the road announced my arrival. I wheeled into the drive that ran between hedgerows and stopped in front of a white house trimmed in yellow shutters and doors. I turned off the roadster and waited for the dog. It came running down a lane to my right, a brown mutt of indeterminate breed. It skidded to a stop outside my roadster and barked and woofed until a lady came to the door of the house and yelled for it to hush. The dog barked once again for good measure and looked to his mistress for approval. It looked back at me. Then, having earned its keep, it turned and trotted back down the lane.

I walked to the door and removed my hat and gave the woman my card.

"Mrs. Egan, please accept my condolences," I said. "I'm a parent, also, and losing a child must be one of life's worst hardships. I'm very sorry."

She nodded and looked at my card.

"The police have been here," she said and gazed over my shoulder. "Don't know that they found anything, though. Didn't act like they did."

"I understand. I'm a private investigator. Is Mr. Egan around?"

She jutted her chin down the lane.

"He's down to the barn, maybe one of the outbuildings. Probably wrestling with that darn tractor of his."

I nodded and thanked her and walked toward the barn. Thunder pealed in the distance, and clouds formed on the western horizon. Sand in the lane crept over my shoe tops as I walked. A smart guy visiting a farmer in the country would have brought along a pair of boots. I had not. Hogs in a pen grunted and snorted when I walked past but lost interest when they saw I didn't carry a bucket of slop. A stack of beehives sat dormant in the weeds. I saw no sign of bees. The barn door was open, and I stepped inside and caught a heady whiff of hay and manure, not an unpleasant aroma. A Holstein cow displayed her rump in one stall, and a horse neighed and stomped in a stall further in. Several cats scurried about, but there was no sign of Mr. Egan.

The shed beyond the barn listed a bit to one side. The rear end of a tractor extended from the double-wide door, and the rear end of a man extended from the tractor. I called out a hello and received a wave of a hand holding a wrench.

"Howdy," he said. "Give me a minute."

He grunted and worked his tools before laying a pair of wrenches atop the tractor and turning to face me.

"What can I do for you?" he said.

The dog I'd encountered earlier rose from the dirt floor and came over and sniffed me from soles to crotch. Egan stood up. I introduced myself and repeated the condolences I'd shared with Mrs. Egan. He nodded and wiped his hands on an oily rag.

"My missus sits up at the house and sifts through pictures of our boy and cries into her hanky. At night she moans in her sleep. Our daughter is bewildered, doesn't know what to do or who to blame. She's lost her brother, and she fears losing her mother. I don't know what to do, either. I hide down here in the shed and tinker with this old devil machine and try not to think about it. Try not to think about my boy dead and buried, about the monster who did this to my family. The police have been here. They've looked around, down to the campsite, along the river. If they found anything, they haven't told us."

"I spoke to the police yesterday," I said. "They haven't solved this crime, but they won't stop until they do. I won't either. I'm working privately, but I share my information with the police."

"You're working privately," Egan said. "That means someone is paying you. Who would that be?"

"It's a man I met recently. He hired me on another matter. When he read about your son's murder in the newspaper, he asked me to investigate, to work with the police but investigate on my own."

"This fella have a name?" he said.

"He docs. He knew your wife's father. Met him when he was in the army. They served together in the Philippines."

"You're speaking of Wil Fallon," he said. "He told us all about their time in the army. My wife never met her father. You probably knew that. From the way Fallon told it, her father never knew she existed. He died before she was born."

"That's the way I heard it, too," I said.

"So, he hired you, huh? I guess I'm not surprised. He's always been a generous fella. Helped care for Katherine's mother before she passed. He came by recently, just before the boys, you know, before that night."

This was news to me. Fallon hadn't mentioned it.

"Why did he come by? Did he do that often?"

"He'd stop by from time to time. Nothing routine, you understand. He said he used the trip to the country as an excuse to clear his head, leave the city behind for a few hours. At least that's what he always told us. He managed to leave a few dollars, too, each time he stopped by. Sometimes more than a few dollars. Like I said, he's generous man. I refused the money at first, but he insisted. Said he did it out of respect for his pal, Red, sort of like a tribute or a memorial, I suppose. I finally quit letting it sting my pride and accepted his gifts. After all, he did it because of my wife, Red's daughter, and we always found a need for the money."

"Did you discuss Fallon's visit with the police?" I said.

"No, it never came up. Why would it?" he said.

"No reason. Tell me about the boys, cousins I understand? Would the other boy, Walter, be your brother's son?"

"That's right."

Egan told me that he and his brother each inherited a quarter section of land that abutted each other. His brother lived at the next place to the east. The Arkansas River ran through each of their farms before making its way to Wichita and beyond. The cousins were born just a few months apart and grew up more like brothers than cousins. They loved farm life and spent many hours together down along the river.

"I'd like to look at the campsite," I said.

Egan stared at the ground and spit.

"You can go along, I guess. Won't hurt nothing. I won't be joining you. I went there with the police and once again after they finished their investigation. I'd rather not return to that spot for a while."

He gave me directions to follow a two-track road through the pasture until I reached the dike.

"Go along the top of the dike to the east until you see the remains of an old cabin down by the river's edge. Drop down there. The campsite is a few yards west of the cabin."

I thanked Egan and turned to walk back to my roadster, but he called me back.

"Better take that old Ford," he said and nodded toward a gray pickup truck that sat in front of the shed. "You might high-center in that rig of yours. The keys are in it."

The trip to the river was short in distance, but between the rutted two-track and the worn springs on the pickup, the trip pounded my backside and jarred my skeleton. I bounced and rocked and swore under my breath and reminded myself to thank Egan for the loan of his truck. My roadster was used to city travel and never would have made this backcountry journey. I pulled up alongside the remains of the cabin, three walls and only a piece of a roof, and walked west to the campsite.

The site was easy to recognize, but I could see that an inspection would yield few clues. Egan said he had returned to the site once after the police investigation. He didn't tell me why, but it was clear what he had done. Sand and mud from the riverbank had been shoveled in to cover much of the site, no doubt to bury the blood left when the body was removed. Ashes from the fire remained, but the firewood had been burned or scattered.

I watched the river roll by and spied a heron poised on a sandbar. How could a setting so tranquil become the scene of a heinous crime? I looked upriver to the west and spotted the bridge I had crossed earlier in my roadster. I also spotted storm clouds gathering and moving closer. A foot trail along the riverbank wound from the campsite toward the bridge. I walked along the trail and looked for anything unusual. I also kept an eye out for snakes. Although temperatures had dropped in October, we still experienced mild weather. Snakes could still be active.

Near the bridge, the trail reached an embankment and ran up to the road above. I climbed the embankment and looked back toward the campsite. A killer, a person with knowledge that the boys would be camping along the river, could easily observe the site from that spot without being noticed. A copse of cottonwood trees along the embankment would provide ample cover for an automobile. A drop of rain fell on the back of my neck and slid down my collar. It was followed by another and another. I took quick steps back down the trail toward the pickup truck.

A thought nagged at me. Fallon just happened to visit the farm right before the campout. It was easy to imagine an excited boy mentioning his upcoming adventure. Had Andrew Egan spoken about it while Fallon was there? Was Fallon aware of the boys' plans? If so, he could easily have stalked the boys that night. But why? What could be his motive? The police hadn't asked about Fallon because at that time they didn't know about Fallon. They didn't know about his relationship with the family. There had been no reason to ask about him. They would find out, though. Thanks to our conversation together, McCormick now knew that

Fallon had an interest in both murders. McCormick would question him. Maybe he already had questioned him. Another coincidence. Another itch to scratch. Too many coincidences, and too many itches. They kept adding up. The total was growing bigger and bigger. The more I added, the less I liked the math.

The Cry of a Hungry Child

The Cry of a Hungry Child

Ralph Waldo came to my office the next afternoon, and he couldn't have chosen a better time to stop in. I sat in my office and read the local news and tried not to listen to the conversation taking place in the outer office. Agnes chatted with Percival Gillman, her betrothed, about their upcoming nuptials, scheduled for only four days away. From their conversation, it sounded like some minor details needed to be ironed out. Agnes told me it was to be a small wedding, only a few friends and relatives in attendance, but it was still a wedding, her wedding, and even the simplest ceremony is special, especially to the bride. I'd give Agnes away. Lucille Hamilton had accepted my invitation to accompany me and be my date for the day.

Although I felt a vague unease, call it jealousy, over Agnes choosing to live her life with Gillman, I knew it was the right move for her. Agnes and I had once shared a brief, passionate romance, but when she came to work for me, we understood that our relationship would have to be business only. That didn't mean that we didn't still care for one another. Gillman was a banker, and he would provide everything for Agnes that I couldn't, stability, a regular paycheck, a secure future—all things that a woman wanted and needed from a man. I idly wondered how my life would be different if I had pursued a more stable career, perhaps in banking or maybe insurance. I'd live by the clock, leave home every day at nine, return home every day at five. Every new day would be much like the day before, the same routine day after day until one day I retired with a pat on the back and a gold watch on my wrist. What a life that would be. I thought of a snared fox and realized I'd rather gnaw off my leg than die in the clutches of a steel trap. No thanks.

Agnes had drawn a red circle around a notice in *The Eagle*. A national authority on feminine charm was in Wichita for several days and would be offering seminars for the modern woman. Janette Serrec suggested that a wise homemaker must be careful of her appearance. Good cooking was not enough to satisfy a man. "A frilly frock may be as important as a delectable doughnut," she was quoted as saying. Serrec would be doling out advice over the next several evenings at the Arcadia Theater for only one thin dime per session. Although Agnes apparently planned on attending, I would wager a buck against her dime that she could teach the expert a thing or two about feminine charm.

Another article mentioned that the Wichita police had questioned a local professor in regard to the two recent stabbings in the area. The article gave Fallon's name and position at the university but only stated that he had known both of the victims. He was not being held, and police were still searching for clues. It said that the police were also working closely with a local private investigator, but no identity was given. There was a call for anyone in the community with information about the murders to contact the police immediately.

The weather report stated that a cold front had come through Kansas the day before. Temperatures dropped twenty degrees in an hour, no news and no surprise to anyone familiar with local weather patterns. Seasons in Kansas changed in an afternoon. A knock on the door announced Ralph Waldo's arrival, and I tossed the paper aside.

"Ralph, good to see you," I said and rose to shake hands.

He took a chair across the desk, and I lit a cigarette. Ralph told me that he'd met with Henry Brown.

"He's not doing well," he said, "but he talked to me. I think he needed to talk to me, to somebody. His sister, his baby sister he still calls her, was really all he had. People used to comment on the way he looked after her, took care of her, you know, and I suspect she gave him a reason to get up in the morning, a reason to live, to keep going. While she was alive, he had a purpose, you know what I mean?"

I assured Ralph I did know.

"Now, he's lost that purpose," he said, "at least that's the way it looks to me. I don't know him well, so I can't speak with certainty."

"I doubt anyone can," I said. "From what we've gathered, no one knew the pair well. They had each other. Maybe Brown has a friend, but if he confided in you, yours may be the only ear he has."

Ralph nodded.

"I asked him about his sister's personal effects," he said. "He showed me her Bible and the necklace you asked about. She got it years ago for perfect attendance in Sunday school. It was just a cheap old thing, but she wore it every day, a silver chain with a small cross attached to it. The chain was broken. Brown found it tucked inside her Bible. You'd asked about a diary, too, and Brown said his sister owned one and wrote it in. He'd never read it, never seen what was inside of it, but he knew she had one. As far as he knows, that's all that is missing."

Ralph went on to say that he'd invited Brown to his parents' home for dinner, and they'd spent a pleasant evening together. Brown had worked as a caretaker at a local cemetery, but while he was in jail, he lost his job to someone else, so he was out of work. Ralph and his dad, Ellis Waldo, vowed to help him find other work. I thanked Ralph, and we moved to the outer office. Percival Gillman had departed. Agnes had an envelope that she handed to Ralph. He smiled and offered his appreciation.

"Thanks, again, Ralph, and give your dad my best," I said.

Agnes cleared her throat and nodded at my shoes. I looked down. Although I'd wiped off much of the dirt and mud from yesterday's visit to the country, after my hike down the river trail, my shoes were in sore need of a shine. Agnes was always right.

"Never mind," I said. "I'll speak to your dad myself."

Agnes smiled approval, and Ralph left.

"Well, hello stranger," Tom said when I walked into the inn bearing his name.

He pulled the stick on the tap and filled a glass with frothy Storz beer. He dropped a coaster on the bar and centered the glass of beer atop it. I took the barstool and heaved a sigh.

"You sound like you need that beer," he said.

"I'm ready for it," I said,

"You haven't been in lately," he said. "Hot on the trail of crime and criminals or just too self-important to remember your old friends?"

"I'm on a trail, alright, one that keeps going in circles. Sometimes I wonder what I'm doing in this lousy business."

"Quit whining," Tom said. "At least you're working. You may have the occasional stretch between paydays, but you can always depend on crime to keep you busy. There's a steady supply. You have enough jingle in your jeans to afford a beer and a sandwich and pleasant company to boot. That's more than many have these days."

"Fair enough," I said. "Why don't you ask that lovely wife of yours to craft one of her specialties for me?"

Tom called for Mabel, and she shuffled from the kitchen.

"Mabel, darling, how about fortifying a hungry soldier? Whatever you suggest is fine with me. I'll leave it in your talented hands," I said.

Mabel patted me on the arm.

"It's good to see you, Pete. I'll fix you a plate."

She shuffled back toward the kitchen. She moved slowly. I looked at Tom and raised an eyebrow.

"I know, I know," he said in a low voice. "I've tried to get her to take a day or two off. Maybe work fewer hours. She won't do it. She says this inn is all she has, and she won't give it up. She loves cooking in that kitchen."

I was worried about Mabel, and I could tell that Tom was, too. She was getting older, and she carried extra pounds. She may be forced to slow down whether she wanted to or not. I drained my beer, and Tom refilled my glass.

"Tell me about these circles you're running in," he said, changing the subject. "Tough case?"

"It's a puzzler," I said. "I guess if they weren't puzzlers, I'd be out of a job."

Tom picked up a copy of the newspaper lying on the bar.

"I was just reading about these recent murders," he said. "Police say they've questioned a university professor. Sounds suspicious to me. Also says they're working with a local gumshoe. I noticed when you came in that your gumshoes have a glossy shine."

"I read that article, too," I said. "There was no mention of a gumshoe. It did, however, mention a private investigator."

"Touchy, touchy," Tom said. "Don't be so sensitive. You know what I'd say to this private investigator, that is, if I knew the guy? I'd tell him to stop running in circles. Slow down. Wait a moment. Sometimes what you think you see isn't what's actually there. Sometimes you look into the shadows and swear you see a ghost. No one in his right mind would believe you, but you're sure that's what you saw. The question is, was the ghost real or not?"

"My grandma used to tell me that," I said.

I thought about Grandma and what she told me as a child. When I was in a hurry, and I was always in a hurry, she'd tell me to slow down, to wait. I thought about a dream I'd had some weeks ago. When she was a young girl, Grandma was sure she had seen a ghost. As a small boy, I was convinced her vision was real. I didn't know if I still believed her story, but I did agree with Tom, that what a person recognized in the shadows often turned out to be something altogether different.

"Let me tell you a story," Tom said.

I lit a cigarette and waited. I was a sucker for Tom's stories.

"This must have been, what? Almost forty years ago, I guess. I was young and not yet married, although Mabel and I were engaged. I'd gone up to Kansas City to see an uncle about working in his tavern. I stayed with him for a few days, considered his offer, but decided I'd rather open a place right here and be my own boss. I hopped on a bus and headed back to Wichita. When the bus left Kansas City, the sun was dropping, and it was coming up a storm. Lightning flashed in the west."

Mabel arrived with a platter that featured a steak sandwich topped with melted cheese and fried onions. The sandwich was surrounded by fried potatoes and dill pickle spears. Mabel stood at my elbow until I took a bite and offered a yum in approval.

"This is delicious," I said, "fit for a king. I wonder what the poor people are eating."

I thanked her, and she smiled and shuffled back to the kitchen. Tom continued his story.

"The bus wasn't full, a dozen or so passengers, and I sat in a pair of empty seats so I could stretch out. I tossed my tote onto the seat next to the window and sat on the aisle across from a soldier in uniform who looked to be about my age. He was reading a dog-eared copy of *Huckleberry Finn*. He held the book about two inches from his nose. I'll never forget that. He glanced over when I sat down and stuck a finger in the book to hold his place. He nodded, and I returned his nod. He seemed open to conversation, and his light was fading, so he could no longer read. I introduced myself. He folded the corner of his page and set the book aside and gave me his name. He told me he'd read *Huck Finn* six or seven times, but it was still his favorite book. We chatted back and forth about nothing important, and we stared out the window at the rolling hills and let the hum of the bus tires fill the gaps in our conversation."

Tom paused to refill my glass and poured one for himself. I glanced around the inn and saw that we were alone.

"About an hour or so out of Kansas City, the bus slowed, on the edge of Ottawa I believe it was, and the driver announced a ten-minute stop to take on new passengers. As soon as the bus came to a stop, a couple of little children a few rows behind us started fussing and whining. I guess they'd been sleeping, and they woke up hungry. Their mother soothed them and hummed and tried to get them back to sleep. I heard her say that they'd be home in the morning, and in the morning they'd have a fine breakfast. Well morning might as well be a year from now to a child with an empty belly. When they heard that, they cried even harder. I glanced back and noticed that the woman held a third child, a tiny baby, asleep in her arms. A flour sack at her feet held their belongings.

"I turned back again, and the soldier wasn't in his seat. It was empty. I saw him at the front of the bus, hunched over and talking to the driver. Their voices were low, but I heard the soldier say something about the woman and her children. He wanted to go to the diner across the street to get something for the children to eat. The soldier thought it might take more than ten minutes, and he was afraid the bus would leave without him. The driver turned and

165

looked down the aisle toward the woman and turned back to the soldier and nodded. 'You go get some food,' he said. 'This bus will be here when you get back.'

"We ended up idling at the stop for over twenty-minutes. The storm rolled in, and the skies opened. The soldier returned to the bus in drenched khakis, but he carried a sack of fried chicken and a loaf of bread and a bottle of milk, and he wore a big grin on his face. Those youngsters smelled that food and lit into it like it was a Thanksgiving feast. I think he even brought some cookies in that sack. He sat back down and looked over at me with a goofy grin. Then his face got all serious. 'You know,' he said, 'I saw all manners of horror in the army, in the Philippines. I saw men mortally wounded from artillery, and I heard men in the throes of death cry like babies for their mamas. I watched one man die in agony from snakebite. But nothing touches me like the cry of a hungry child. I can't abide it, and I won't abide it if I can do something about it.'

"I just nodded. The bus rolled along in the rain, and I lay back and closed my eyes. Sometime later, I sensed movement, and I saw the soldier had left his seat. He moved back toward the woman. She had fallen asleep and so had her children. Her handbag was at her feet. The soldier picked up her bag and opened it and removed her wallet. I watched him take several bills out of his pocket, his mustering out pay, I suppose. He stuffed the money inside her wallet. I turned to the front and noticed the bus driver looking in his mirror, watching what took place. I closed my eyes and slept the rest of the way.

"We got to Wichita, and it was dark and raining hard. Passengers stirred and gathered their belongings. The driver looked in his mirror and called for the soldier to come to the front of the bus. He moved forward, and the two men huddled and nodded. When the bus arrived downtown, the driver didn't turn toward the station. Instead, he kept going and crossed over the river. We stopped at a house on Second Street several blocks west of downtown. The soldier and I shook hands and said our goodbyes. Then he shook hands with the driver and got off the bus. The driver delivered that soldier right to his doorstep.

"I never spoke to that man again. Never saw him. Our paths didn't cross, even though we both live here in Wichita. He and I have little in common. He went back to school like he promised himself he would, and Mabel and I married and opened this place. Like the proverbial two ships, that soldier and I just passed each other in the night. Still, I never forgot the man's decency, his tenderness toward that mother and her children, people he didn't even know. We never saw one another again, but I never forgot his name. I recently read it in the newspaper. That soldier's name was Wil Fallon."

It All Went Dark
Iͼ ΛΙΙ ΜͼUͼ ᗡꟻꟽK

"Every clue I've uncovered points to only one person as a suspect, and that person is Wil Fallon. It doesn't add up, and yet it does add up. Fallon knew both of the victims. He's the common thread between the two. He not only knew the victims, he was involved in the lives of both. One was a student at the university. The other was a child from out in the county. As far as I can tell, the two had nothing in common other than a mutual association with Wil Fallon. They probably never crossed paths with each other. Why would they? They were unknown to one another. I can't believe Fallon is guilty. I don't want to believe Fallon is guilty. Yet, every time I go over the facts, the arrow points in the same direction, to the same person—Wil Fallon."

The story Tom told me the night before left me puzzled. On the one hand, those who knew Wil Fallon spoke of his kindness and generosity. He seemed to be a person willing to lend a hand to a fellow traveler down on his luck. He was a person to be admired. On the other hand, at least two people who knew Fallon, two people Fallon had helped, were now dead. The only connection between the two was Fallon himself. I needed to talk to someone other than the police, someone who knew Fallon better than I did.

"Hang on to those doubts you have about Fallon's guilt, Pete. Don't let them go. Fallon is a good man. I believe that. He didn't commit these crimes. Wil isn't capable of such dastardly behavior."

The speaker was Ethan Alexander, Wichita University professor of history. Alexander had mentored my son when he was a student at the university. Alexander had also helped me on a previous case involving the murders of several city policemen. When Fallon sought advice on selecting a detective, it was Alexander who had recommended me. He had agreed to meet me early Thursday morning, before classes started and most of the faculty and students arrived, to discuss the case and share his thoughts on Fallon's character.

We sat in Alexander's office. He puffed on his pipe, and I smoked a cigarette. The cold front and rainstorm had passed through to the east, leaving clear skies over the city. Alexander opened his window, and a breeze freshened the room.

"Okay, let's agree that Fallon is innocent," I said. "Never mind that the police have talked with him and may suspect him. If Fallon is innocent, someone must want him to look guilty. The question is who? Who stands to gain if Fallon is out of the picture, locked up or executed for murder?"

Alexander looked over my shoulder and puffed on his pipe.

"I suppose we both know the answer to that question," he said. "This is your area, Pete. You'll have to say it. I'm unaccustomed to pointing a finger at another person and uttering J'accuse."

"The only person I can think of is Muriel Fallon, his wife."

"Bingo," he said and nodded.

"But why? For the money? I met her when I visited Fallon's home. She looks to be living the life of ease."

"She's younger than Wil," he said. "Maybe she's found some-one else, someone she'd like to be with, but she's reluctant to leave the security marriage to Fallon offers."

"I still don't like her for the killer," I said. "It makes no sense. Why the elaborate ruse, the murders of innocent victims? It doesn't fit. It can't be the wife. If she wanted Fallon out of the way, all she'd have to do is add a little rat poison to his soup. No, someone's trying to make a statement. She wouldn't have to kill innocent people."

Even as I spoke the words, I didn't believe them, and I could see that Alexander didn't believe them either. An elaborate ruse would be just the thing to draw attention away from Mrs. Fallon, whereas poisoning her husband in their home would lead the po-lice right to her as the sole suspect. On the other hand, hiring a detective to solve a double murder would be an excellent way to draw attention away from oneself, to convince the detective and the police that you were not a suspect, just as Dr. Fallon had done by hiring me.

When I left Alexander's office, I was at sea, floundering in deep water and unable to come up with a name or a face or a clue as to who could be a logical suspect. My time with the history pro-fessor wasn't wasted, however. He was yet another associate who attested to Fallon's generosity and goodwill toward others, a man who could never be suspected of murder. Why, then, did I still harbor doubts as to his character?

When I got in my roadster, I noticed Fallon's tan Hudson parked nearby, but I hadn't seen him and doubted if he'd noticed me. The campus had more activity at mid-morning than it did when I arrived. Students and faculty alike have an aversion to early morning classes. I drove on reflex, giving little thought to my ac-tions.

I was lost in thought and drifted south from the university. When I reached the College Hill Park area, I pulled up in front of a house on Fountain Street, a tall, white colonial with a burgundy door and matching shutters. The first time I'd been to this home was during the evening, and I hadn't seen it well from the street. Sculpted shrubs and bright chrysanthemums, white and gold and violet, were arrayed in beds on either side of the columned entryway. An oak tree stood to one side of the walk with a trio of maples clustered on the other side, all ablaze in fall colors. A few leaves lay scattered on the trimmed lawn.

I hadn't let Dr. Fallon know that I was going to visit his wife. If Fallon wanted me to investigate, I'd have to do it my way. I didn't call ahead for an appointment because I didn't want Mrs. Fallon to be prepared for my questions. I knew Fallon was at the university campus, and I suspected that Mrs. Fallon would be at home during the morning hours. I strolled up the walk and used the brass knocker on the front door, and in a few moments Mrs. Fallon opened the door. She was dressed in a floor-length, crème colored housecoat that probably cost more than the suit on my back along with the others in my closet. She wore no make-up or jewelry, but her soft brown hair was brushed to a sheen, and her green eyes danced. She had looked attractive on my first visit. That morning she was radiant.

"Mr. Stone, how nice to see you again. Are you looking for Wil? I'm afraid he's left for the university."

"Actually, Mrs. Fallon, I was hoping to speak to you. Could you give me a few moments, please?"

"Me? You wish to speak to me?" she said and flashed a coquettish grin. "I can't imagine what you'd want to speak to me about, but you've aroused my curiosity. Do come in."

She stepped aside, and I removed my hat and went through the doorway. She led me through the kitchen. A used cup and saucer lay in the sink, and a pleasant aroma wafted from the oven. We entered a breakfast nook, and she offered me a seat at the table. A half-filled coffee cup rested on a saucer, and a cigarette burned in an ashtray. She reached over and snuffed it out. I was surprised to see the cigarette. I recalled Fallon's comment that smoke bothered his wife's sinuses.

"Will you join me in a cup of coffee?" she said. "I have sweet rolls baking in the oven. Feel free to smoke. Dear Wil doesn't approve of my cigarettes, but he thinks I don't know when he sneaks a cigar in his study. It's a silly game we play. Men are so naïve about the women in their lives. They think we are so innocent and unaware. It's male ignorance that gives us women power. What are your thoughts? Is there a Mrs. Stone?"

"Not at the moment," I said.

She smiled, and I thanked her for the coffee. I took a sip and lit a cigarette. I offered one to her, but she declined.

"Mrs. Fallon," I said, and she interrupted me.

"Please call me Muriel," she said. "May we use first names? I feel so old when people call me Mrs. Fallon."

"Very well, I'm Pete. Muriel, your husband has hired me to solve, or at least to assist the police in solving, recent murders. Has he discussed this with you?"

"I knew when you came to our home that night that he was upset about the murder of his former student, Miss Cleveland. When the police released that young man, their suspect, I asked Wil what that meant, and he seemed pleased by the news. I found that odd. I thought he wanted justice. He assured me that he did want justice, but the real killer has yet to be found. Is that why you're working for my husband? So you can find the real killer?"

"Yes, that's right."

She sipped her coffee and placed her cup gently on its saucer.

"You said murders," she said.

"Are you aware of the murder of the young boy near Mt. Hope, the lad on a camping trip?"

"Yes, yes, I read about that, and I know Wil spoke to the police. He knew the boy's family. What does that mean?"

"That's why I'm here," I said.

A chime in the kitchen interrupted our discussion. She excused herself and returned a few moments later with a plate of cinnamon rolls. I declined her offer of a roll but accepted a refill of coffee. She took a small bite and asked me to go on.

"That's why I'm here," I said again. "The two murders are similar in nature, and the police suspect they were committed by the same person. So far, the only person I've discovered to have a connection to both victims is your husband. The police have questioned your husband. They will draw similar conclusions."

Muriel's eyes widened.

"Are you suggesting that my husband is a murderer?" she said. She covered her mouth with her napkin and laughed into it. "Wil? A killer? You can't be serious."

"If it helps, I don't believe your husband is the murderer, but the evidence points in his direction. What I think doesn't matter. As I say, the police have questioned him. They don't have definitive proof of his guilt. You can bet they are looking for proof. Has he said anything to you about that?"

"Well, yes, I know the police questioned him, but I had no idea he was a suspect. Wil acted unconcerned, like he wanted to help the police in any way he could. If the police suspect my husband, why hasn't he been arrested?"

"So far, the evidence is circumstantial. Police need more concrete evidence. They are also looking for a motive. Why would he or anyone else want two innocent people killed?"

She shook her head. I lit another cigarette and offered one to Muriel, but she declined.

"Are you aware of your husband's financial situation?" I said. "From what he's told me, you are pretty well off. From what I've gathered in my investigation, he's also generous."

A brief frown appeared on her face, and it lost a bit of radiance.

"Yes, he's generous," she said and stared into her coffee cup.

"You don't seem pleased by that," I said.

She met my eyes and smiled.

"You've surely noticed that I'm younger than my husband. There's every possibility that I will live a long while after he is gone. Wil treats me well, and I've grown accustomed to a comfortable lifestyle, but will that lifestyle continue after my husband is gone? Will there be any money left after he's gone? I don't know. I don't mean to sound greedy, but a woman becomes accustomed to living life in a certain way. I'm merely concerned about my future."

Muriel Fallon was a beautiful woman, but she was also a calculating woman. I suspected her beauty ran skin deep.

"If I were alone, I guess I could remarry," she said. "Perhaps a man younger than Wil would find me attractive."

She placed her fingertips on my wrist. I raised my arm to sip my coffee, and her fingertips fell away.

"Perhaps," I said. "Does your husband share his financial information with you? Do you know where the money goes?"

"No, not really. He only tells me not to worry. He tells me to enjoy my life and let him take care of the details."

I doubted that was entirely true. Fallon may have told his wife not to worry, but I suspected Muriel would have gone through his financial records herself.

"Do you know anyone who might have reason to kill two people," I said, "two people known to your husband?"

"No, I don't. I'm sorry I can't be of more help."

I sensed our talk was over and rose from my chair. She reached for my arm and leaned into me and escorted me to the door. Her radiance was back for a return engagement.

"I do hope to see you again," she said and squeezed my arm. "Maybe we can talk about something other than these nasty old murders."

"Sure," I said. "We can talk of many things, like cabbages and kings, and whether pigs have wings."

She gave me an odd look. I released my arm from hers and put on my hat and stepped over the threshold. The door closed behind me. I stood on the step for a moment and pondered my discussion with Muriel Fallon. Were her flirtations innocent? Was she greedy or simply bored in her marriage? Maybe Ethan Alexander was right. Maybe she had found another man. Maybe she was shopping for one. I stood by my earlier assessment, however. She may have been calculating, but I couldn't picture Muriel Fallon as the killer.

I heard stirring from the bushes behind me and started to turn, but I never got a chance. Someone leapt toward me, and a sap landed at the base of my skull. I didn't see who it was. I dropped backwards into a pair of arms and caught the fiery blaze of leaves overhead before it all went dark.

What You Hired Me to Do

"Stone! Mr. Stone! Pete. Can you hear me?"

I eased out of the darkness into a splendid bright flame. I probed the back of my head with my fingertips. It felt like a melon someone had dropped.

"I think he's coming around."

The voice was masculine. I was lying on my back and struggled to get my feet under me, but hands held me down.

"Don't try to stand yet. Just sit for a moment. Here, drink this."

I swallowed water from a glass and focused my eyes. I was seated on the ground among a bed of flowers, mums it appeared. Evergreen shrubs brushed my face. My neck and head ached.

"You must have fallen and hit your head. You've got quite a bruise on the back of your head and neck."

I looked up toward the speaker and discovered it was Wil Fallon. Muriel Fallon hovered over his shoulder and frowned. I took in my surroundings. I was sitting among the shrubs and flowers next to the Fallon house, not far from the front porch.

"I didn't fall," I said. "Someone hit me."

A cool damp cloth appeared, and Fallon placed it behind my head.

"Someone hit you? How could that be? Are you sure? Who would have done something like that? Maybe you're imagining things, hallucinating. We'd better get you to a doctor. I can drive you."

The drink of water and the cool towel helped bring me around. I got my bearings and stood up with Fallon's help.

"No, I'm feeling better now. I'll go slowly. Thanks anyway."

"You really should let me take you to a doctor. You need medical attention."

Maybe I should have accepted his offer of driving me to a doctor, but even in my condition, I couldn't shake the feeling that Fallon had done this to me. One minute I was knocked out cold, and the next minute I was staring into Fallon's face. I wasn't thinking clearly yet, but I knew I had to get out of there.

"Mr. Stone, why are you here, anyway?" he said. "What were you doing?"

"I was about to ask you the same question," I said.

Fallon looked perturbed.

"You were about to ask me what I am doing here? Why, I live here! This is my home. I came home for lunch, not that it's any of your business. I'll ask you again. What are you doing at my home?"

"I'm doing what you hired me to do," I said. "I'm investigating two murders."

I picked my hat up off the ground and stood as straight as I was able and eased down the walk to my car. I may have weaved. Looking back later, my memories of the next several minutes were clouded. Although I recalled no details, I drove downtown because my roadster was parked at the curb outside the Lawrence Block Building on Douglas. The elevator boy called out my name when I crossed the lobby. For reasons I couldn't explain, I ignored the elevator and shuffled up the stairs to my office. I opened the door, and Agnes looked at me and gasped. I slumped into a chair.

Agnes was a trooper. She acted just as she always did in a crisis—address the problem first and ask questions later. She left the
room and returned in a moment with a glass of water and a wet
towel. She fed me a pair of white tablets and held the glass for me
while I swallowed the water. Then she placed the damp towel behind my head and neck and held it in place. Her touch was gentle,
but the tone of her voice was not.

"Okay, buster, let's have it. What gives? Who did this and
why?"

I started to speak, but she stopped me.

"Wait a minute. Look at me. I want to see your eyes."

She held the towel behind my head with one hand and used
the other to turn my head toward hers. Our eyes met, and our
noses were inches apart.

"Why, Agnes, darling, does this mean what I think it does?
Are you throwing over Percival the banker in favor of yours truly?
My heart longs for you."

"Keep quiet, you moron," she said. "I'm trying to see if your
pupils are dilated or uneven."

She looked into my eyes then leaned behind me and looked
under the towel. She smelled like lilacs, and I said so. She shook
her head.

"Even with a knock to the noggin you make a pass at a girl.
You're incorrigible. Your eyes look fine, but that knot on the back
of your head is as big as a baseball. I'm putting you on the bench
for the rest of the day. You can just abandon any thoughts you
have of fighting crime until that swelling goes down. I'm taking
you out of the game."

"Okay, coach, okay."

"Now give. What happened?"

I told Agnes about my visit to the Fallon home, about my talk
with Muriel Fallon.

"She's a piece of work, alright. I concluded that Muriel Fallon is a gold digger living on easy street, but that doesn't make her guilty of a crime. She's hardly the only woman who fits that description. The jury is out on whether she's involved in the murders. We finished our discussion and said our goodbyes, and I stepped out onto the porch. The next thing I knew I was lying toes up in the flower bed with her husband the professor standing over me. He also gave me a glass of water and a cool towel, by the way, but looking into his eyes wasn't nearly as pleasant as gazing into yours."

"Like I said—incorrigible."

"I'll be in my office," I said. "Say, I haven't eaten anything today. I could use some nourishment. Would you make a call, please? Have the hotel send something up. Anything's fine."

I entered my office and closed the door. I sat down at my desk and put up my feet. The sounds of Agnes on the phone came through the door, but I couldn't hear what she ordered. It didn't matter.

I picked up a newspaper and glanced at the headlines and read an article about an oddball called Daredevil Dault who entertained audiences with acrobatic stunts. The paper reported that he had wowed a crowd at the fairgrounds the day before with his latest feat. He stacked three card tables atop a Ferris wheel and placed four small bottles on the top table. He then stacked a pair of chairs on the bottles and took a seat on the upper chair. All of this was done without a safety net. The guy must have been so high up I doubted he could have heard the applause. It gave me the shivers. I made a mental note to show the article to Agnes. And she thought I lived dangerously.

The Wichita Shockers football team were three and one and would travel to South Dakota for Saturday's game. I tossed the paper aside and mulled over my visit with Muriel Fallon. When I walked through her kitchen, I noticed a used cup and saucer in the sink. I assumed the professor had used the dishes before he left home that morning. Maybe I was wrong. Maybe someone else visited the Fallon house just before I did. I was also puzzled by the burning cigarette in the ashtray. Had that belonged to Muriel? Muriel claimed she smoked without her husband's knowledge, but the professor had told me earlier that he confined his cigar smoking to his study because the fumes bothered his wife's sinuses. Muriel hadn't smoked the cigarette in the ashtray. Instead, she crushed it out and later refused my offer of another one. Had the cigarette belonged to an earlier visitor? If she was lying to me, and someone else was with her when I arrived, who could that person be? And was her visitor the person who had knocked me out on the porch? Maybe I jumped to a hasty conclusion by suspecting the professor of hitting me. Questions bothered me, but thinking was difficult. My head ached.

I started to nod off, maybe I dozed, but I started when I heard voices in the outer office, both feminine. My door opened without a knock, and Agnes came in with another woman following her.

"He needs food, rest, and looking after," Agnes said. "Come to think of it, all men do. He thinks he's going back to work today, but I assured him that he is going to rest until the swelling from the bump on his head goes down."

"Don't worry, Agnes, and thanks for calling me. I'll take care of him."

I looked up at Lucille and managed a puzzled smile.

"What are you doing here?" I said, although her presence was becoming clear. Agnes had called her. "Is this a conspiracy? All I asked for was a little chow."

"I'll feed you," Lucille said, "then you're going straight to bed."

I raised my eyebrows.

"You're going to bed to get some rest, Romeo," Lucille said. "Don't get any wise ideas."

"You're incorrigible," Agnes said for the third time.

I grinned, Lucille shook her head, and Agnes rolled her eyes.

That Same World of Violence

That Same World of Violence

"Rise and shine, crime fighter."

The smell of fresh coffee wafted toward my nostrils. Lucille waved the cup near my face and smiled when I opened my eyes. She stood beside the bed, bent over me.

"Now, that's an alarm clock I could get used to," I said.

She leaned over and kissed me on the forehead and handed me the cup.

"Breakfast is almost ready. You don't have to wear a dress shirt to the table, but I do insist on pants."

She kissed me again and left the room. A quick scan made it clear that I was in Lucille's bedroom. I lifted the covers and saw that I was in my skivvies. My suit hung in an open closet, and my shirt and tie were folded on a chair with my hat perched on top. I put the coffee cup on the night table and slipped into my pants and shirt. I walked down the hall to the toilet and noticed the couch in the living room had been made up with sheets and a pillow. The smell of bacon followed me down the hall, and I realized I was ravenous. A few minutes later, I made my way to the kitchen holding my empty cup.

"Say, you sure know how to treat a fellow. That coffee was delicious, and the bacon smells even better. I feel like I haven't eaten in days."

Lucille looked lovely. She wore a pink housedress with a blue floral print beneath a yellow apron. The sun shone through an east window and highlighted her blonde curls. She stood at the stove and worked the frying bacon with a fork.

"You haven't eaten in days," she said, "or at least you didn't eat yesterday from what I gather."

I refilled my cup from the pot on the stove and took a chair at the table.

"Well, what you gather is a whole lot more than what I remember," I said. "How about filling me in on the details? I'm still fuzzy. The last thing I remember is leaning on you as we left the office."

"I think that was the last time you were fully conscious," she said, "right up until this morning. I drove you here, but you fell asleep in the car. You came awake long enough to stagger into the house with my help. I told you to lie down while I made you something to eat, but when I checked on you again, you were out cold on top of my bed. I left you there and slept on the couch."

"I wasn't dressed when I woke up this morning."

Lucille blushed.

"Well, I didn't want your suit to get wrinkled. Getting you out of your clothes was the hardest part. You didn't help at all."

"I'm sorry. Next time you get me out of my clothes, I'll try to be more cooperative," I said.

She blushed again.

"Agnes is right. You're incorrigible."

I was encouraged by her smile. She finished the bacon and scrambled some eggs while I made the toast and poured the orange juice. It tasted even better than it smelled. We ate it all, although I downed the lion's share. I was beginning to feel whole again. Afterward, we lingered and chatted over coffee and cigarettes.

"I'm not trying to pry," she said, "but I assume this bump on your head is related to a case you're working on. Is that correct?"

I nodded.

"Yes, I'm sure it is," I said, "but how it's related isn't clear to me yet. I intend to find out."

"Suppose next time the assailant uses something more lethal than a club. Suppose he—"

"—or she."

"—or she. Suppose he or she uses a knife or a gun. What then, Pete? What happens then?"

"Then I will use my powers of intelligence, fortitude, and strength to overcome the villain, save the damsel in distress, and win the day."

"You mean like you did yesterday?"

"Ouch. That stings."

Lucille reached over and placed her fingertips on my wrist.

"I'm serious, Pete. Don't make jokes. I don't know if I can handle this. I care about you. I've cared about you for some time, but this is different. I'm starting to have strong feelings for you, feelings that I've battled, but I'm losing the fight, and I'm scared."

She squeezed my wrist.

"I think I'm falling in love with you, but I'm afraid. I'm so very afraid. I lost a husband to violence. I know that was something I'll never get over. All I can do is try to live with it. Now I find myself falling for a man who lives in a world of violence every day. I don't know if I could let myself fall in love with a man who lives in that world. What if you were killed? I couldn't lose another man to violence. I'd die myself. I don't know what to do."

"You live in that same world of violence," I said. "We all do. We all live in a violent world. The only difference is that it's my job to face that violence, to bring a little justice into my corner of the world. It's what I do, Lucille. For the record, I've fallen in love with you, too. I want you, and I want us to be together, but I'm

185

not going to push you. I want you to come to me with open eyes and understanding. Just don't assume I'm in constant danger because I'm not. Much of what I do is boring and ordinary. I'm just a Joe like any other trying to make my way in the world as best I can."

We chatted some more, and I glanced at the clock on the kitchen wall. The morning was nearly gone. I had to get back to work. I finished getting dressed and hugged Lucille and thanked her for taking care of me.

"Let's not make any decisions today," I said. "Let's keep seeing each other. Don't forget that you're my date for Agnes's wedding the day after tomorrow."

"I haven't forgotten. I look forward to it."

We parted with a hug and a kiss.

The Books Cried Out
The Books Cried Out

"I must say that I'm more than a little upset with you and your investigation, Mr. Stone. I'm no detective. I don't pretend to know how you operate your business, but I am very displeased by your actions yesterday. Muriel gave me the gist of what occurred at my home—your unannounced visit, your interrogation of my wife and your subsequent accident on my front porch. Most disturbing. I'd like to hear your explanation."

It was the midafternoon on Friday, and I was sitting across the desk from Professor Wilfred Fallon. The window to his office was open, and the fan hummed. After leaving Lucille, I went to my place on Lewellen and cleaned up and changed clothes. I called Fallon's office and told him I wanted to meet with him. He was anxious to meet with me, too, and invited me to come to his office as soon as possible. He was irate at finding me at his home after talking to his wife, but I was the guy with a bump on his head, and I had some gripes myself. I let Fallon have his say before I spoke.

"In the first place, what happened on your porch was no accident. I did not slip and fall. As I tried to explain yesterday, although I may have slurred, someone hit me on the back of the head, someone who had been lying in wait in the bushes, no doubt. I don't know who that person was, of course, but I will

187

know by the time my investigation is completed. Obviously, some-one wants me off the case. That's good news. That means someone is worried that I'm getting too close. You were the person who dis-covered me lying in the flowerbed, professor. Another coincidence on a growing list. I thought you were the culprit who hit me."

"Preposterous."

"Maybe. Maybe not. The people who know you vouch for your character. They seem convinced that you are incapable of murder. I've been around crime long enough to know that anyone under the right circumstances is capable of the most heinous acts. Let the courts assume each man is innocent until proven guilty. A detective assumes anyone may be guilty until proven innocent. Frankly, I don't think you are guilty, but I do know that the evidence points to you as a likely candidate. If you are innocent, then someone must want you to look guilty, someone who would want you out of the way. The question is, who, and why?"

"And you thought that person might be my wife?"

"Possibly. Again, I don't know. At this point your wife is on a short list of suspects. I needed to talk to her, and it was important that I talk to her without announcing my arrival ahead of time, to her or to you. I didn't want her to be prepared for my visit."

"What exactly did you learn from your visit?"

"Nothing definitive. She revealed concern about your ability to provide for her future. For a woman living in luxury, she's awfully worried about where the next dollar will come from."

Fallon shook his head.

"Money, always money," he said. "I've assured her a number of times that money is not a problem. I have enough money to sup-port her if she lives to be a hundred. Is that all you learned, that my wife loves money and the luxuries it affords?"

"No. The person who clobbered me was waiting outside your home. Your wife had just closed the door, so she couldn't have done it."

"Well, that's a relief," he said.

"Remember, an investigation not only uncovers the guilty party, but it eliminates those who are innocent along the way."

"Does that mean that Muriel is innocent?"

"No, it means your wife didn't hit me. Someone else did. That raises a question. Did your wife know that there was someone waiting in the bushes? Is she innocent of the crimes or is she working in collusion with another party? I don't know the answer to those questions."

There was a knock at the door, and a student secretary entered and handed a note to Dr. Fallon. He read it quickly and rose from his desk.

"You'll have to excuse me, but I've been summoned to the dean's office. I shouldn't be gone long. You're welcome to wait here until I return. If you decide to leave call me later, and we'll continue our discussion. Feel free to read something while you wait."

Fallon left the office, and I glanced at the spines of the books lining the shelves. Lots of good literature but hardly anything to be read in a few moments time. A manuscript lay on his desk. I read the title and realized it was the same manuscript that I had seen on his desk the day I met Dr. Landis, "Shakespeare and the Four Humors." A subtitle read, "A Study of the Influence of Greek Philosophy on Shakespeare's Plays." It looked like dry reading, but I picked it up and thumbed through its pages.

The first section of the paper delivered a brief history of the four bodily humors as defined by the Greeks, melancholic, phlegmatic, choleric, and sanguine. The Greeks identified the humors by certain qualities, such as the age of a person, the individual's body organs, as well as the four physical elements, earth, fire, wind, and water. Much of the paper was devoted to Shakespeare's writing and identifying references to bodily humors in his work. Fallon analyzed plays including *Hamlet* and *The Taming of the Shrew* and others. An extensive list of references made up the remainder of the paper. I made some notes in my book thinking they might make interesting conversation with someone more familiar with Shakespeare's plays than I, Ellis Waldo, perhaps.

I looked at my watch. Fallon had been gone over thirty minutes, and I was growing restless. I decided to leave and call him later. I rose from my chair and turned toward the door, and something caught my eye. In a row of books on a shelf near the doorway, several books were crooked and extended forward beyond the others in the row. They seemed to be out of place. I never would have noticed that on another bookshelf, Dr. Alexander's, for example, or even my own at home. I often stack books in a haphazard fashion. However, in an office as neat and orderly as Fallon's, the books cried out to be straightened and put into their proper places. I reached toward the shelf and pushed the spines of the disorderly editions, but I met resistance. I pushed again with the same result, so I removed the books from the shelf and saw that something lay behind them, another book. I removed it and returned the others to their proper positions before I read the cover of the hidden volume. Its two word title was printed in capital letters—MY DIARY.

I took a breath and turned the cover. The frontispiece was an illustration of an angel hovering over an individual, and on the right-hand page were hand-written words in ink, "This diary is presented in love and gratitude to Rosemary Joy Cleveland for her kindness and devotion in caring for Mother during her final days." It was signed and dated January first of that year, nearly ten months earlier.

I closed the cover and slipped the book into my coat pocket and left Fallon's office.

Swallowed by Shadows

"Another beer, Pete?"

"Better make it coffee," I said.

Tom took away my empty plate and beer glass and returned a few moments later with a cup of coffee. The crowd in the inn had thinned, and the remaining few had grown quiet.

"You're not very entertaining company tonight," he said. "What's that you've got your nose stuck into? Is it more interesting than my company? Take time to say hello to your pal for crying out loud."

It was late Friday night, and I sat on a barstool at Tom's Inn. After I left Fallon's office, I went straight to my office downtown. Agnes's sister, who would be her maid of honor on Sunday, had arrived from Salina. The two women were as excited as sorority sisters, laughing and hugging and sharing tales of love and gossip. I told Agnes to take the rest of the day off and shooed them both out the door with assurances that I would be at the church on time for the gala event.

Alone in my office, I pored over Rosemary Joy's diary. The book was a gift from a grateful former employer, and Rosemary Joy had written in it faithfully. Most of the entries were given over to the thoughts and dreams of a young woman trying to find her way in the world with comments on her relationships with friends

191

and her brother, Peanut. She mentioned Peanut often and worried about his struggles to find work and form a stable relationship with a woman. She thought about her friend, Ida Mae Parsons, and hoped that her move to Emporia would improve her prospects for a good education and future employment.

She wrote about her church and her faith. Friends from Calvary Baptist Church picked her up each Sunday and drove her to services on Water Street. Entries from the spring of that year indicated that she'd been attracted to a young man at the church, an oil field roughneck. However, his work had taken him to the oil fields in El Dorado, not far from Wichita but far enough that he attended church with less and less regularity, and by the summer she rarely saw him again.

Rosemary Joy cited several Bible verses in her diary, including the familiar John 3:16, "For God so loved the world . . ." as well as the entire twenty-third Psalm, "The Lord is my shepherd; I shall not want . . ." Occasionally she drew an illustration of a cross and dedicated one page to an illustration of three crosses on a hill.

Later entries indicated possible questions regarding her faith. She wrote cryptic entries, such as, "My Faith?" "My Friend?" "MF?" and illustrations of crosses followed by question marks. These must have been made during a troubling time in her life. I made notes of these entries in my book.

The most troubling passage in the diary came on its final page, penned in a hand unlike Rosemary Joy's. The entry was a crude rhyme and an obvious threat:

"From one's corpus
Spirit doth cleave,
Swallowed by shadows
On All Hallows' Eve."

A chill came over me. The rhyme had been written by the killer and suggested that a final murder, a climax, would be executed on Halloween. At least that was the way I interpreted it. Did Fallon pen the threat and hide the diary on his shelf? Possibly, but it seemed unlikely. If I took the diary to the police and told them where I found it, they would arrest Fallon immediately. If he turned out to be innocent, the killer would still be free. If the killer's objective was to get Fallon out of the way, the murders might very well stop, but justice would go unserved. I looked over my notes and agonized over my dilemma when Tom interrupted me.

"Hello?"

"Sorry, Tom," I said. "My head isn't here tonight. Thinking about a case."

I closed my book and tucked it into my jacket.

"That's what I figured," he said. "You've hardly said a word since you walked in here. Ordered a beer and food. Opened that book of yours and forgot everything else. You didn't even tell Mabel how good her cooking is."

I looked around for Mabel.

"Don't worry. She'll survive," he said. "Does all this concentration of yours have to do with those murders? Cops say they're connected, right?"

"Yeah, it looks like it. I've uncovered some new evidence, evidence that I should take to the police, but I'm reluctant to do it. I'm afraid they'll arrest the wrong guy. I think the evidence may have been planted."

"So, what are you going to do?" he said.

Mabel shuffled out of the kitchen. She fumbled with the buttons on her sweater and called out to Tom that she was going home. Her voice was weak, and her words weren't clear. I could see that the buttons and holes didn't match properly, and her sweater hung askew. I slid off the stool to give her a hand and thank her for the meal she had prepared earlier. Tom sensed something wasn't right and came around the bar. We reached Mabel together and each took an arm. She looked from one face to the other as if she didn't recognize either one of us. She tried to speak, but her words were slurred and didn't make sense. Tom held her under her arms, and I pulled a chair from a table and placed it beneath her to keep her from slumping to the floor.

"Wha, wha?" she muttered.

I ran behind the bar and dialed the telephone. Tom held her hand and spoke softly to her. After I hung up the phone, I poured a glass of water for her to drink. She swallowed some, but much of it ran out of her mouth and down her face. The few remaining customers left their tables and dropped some bills on the bar and went out the door. When the ambulance arrived, Tom and I stepped back and let them do their job. Tom identified himself as the husband and answered questions while they took Mabel's vital signs and strapped her to a gurney. When they had her ready, they rolled the gurney out the door toward the ambulance. Tom tossed me the keys to the inn and followed them out. I put the money in the till and finished cleaning up the place before I hung the "Closed" sign in the window and locked the door behind me.

It was a stroke. It took the doctor no time at all to diagnose the problem. Tom sat bent over in a chair in the hallway. Medical personnel attended to Mabel on the other side of the door. I took a chair next to Tom and wrapped an arm around his shoulders and tried to console him.

"I should have seen this coming," he said. "For weeks now I've been telling Mabel to slow down, to rest. It's all my fault."

"It's not your fault," I said. "We both noticed that she was slowing down. You couldn't have predicted this. She's stubborn and has her pride, and you've said more than once yourself, that kitchen keeps her alive. It gives her life purpose. Running that kitchen is what she does. It's who she is. Stay strong, Tom. She's going to pull through this, and when she does, she's going to need you more than ever."

Nurses in starched white uniforms entered and left the room. We were at the Wichita Hospital and School for Nurses a few blocks south of the inn. The hospital provided a training ground for the students who were not in short supply. Tom asked for information on Mabel's condition, and each time a young lady told him that the doctor would speak to him soon. Eventually, a doctor did appear. Tom rose from his chair, but the doctor told him to remain seated and pulled up another chair facing Tom so he could speak to him directly.

"There's bad news and some good news," the doctor said. "Your wife has suffered a stroke, but we have her stabilized. The next forty-eight hours are crucial. If she doesn't suffer another stroke during that period, her prognosis is favorable. We'll keep her under surveillance. Thankfully, she got to the hospital quickly. From what I gather, you called right away, and you were not far from the hospital. Emergency personnel brought her in with minimal delay. That's always good in cases like this. There's a strong possibility that she will recover, but the extent of her recovery remains to be seen. Even with recovery, however, her life, and yours no doubt, will have to change dramatically. I'll have a nurse coach you on changes in diet and so forth when the time comes. For now, we will watch and do what we can. Do you have any questions?"

Tom and I tried to absorb what the doctor said until Tom finally shook his head and thanked the doctor who nodded and rose from his chair and moved down the hall. I sat with Tom for several hours while Mabel rested in her room. When a nurse appeared and said that Mabel was asking for her husband, I squeezed Tom's hand and patted him on the back. He brushed at a tear with the back of his hand and went through the door to Mabel. I found the exit and drove to my place on Lewellen.

◆ ◆ ◆

Cat Got Your Tongue?

Cat Got Your Tongue?

Agnes looked beautiful in white. Her dark curls fell across her shoulders in stark and stunning contrast to her gown, and even beneath her veil her eyes sparkled. The long train of her dress flowed behind her, carried by a pair of young girls, her nieces I learned. I offered a brave smile when she looped her arm into mine, and we moved down the aisle to organ notes of the traditional Wedding March. The guests rose as we walked by. Agnes looked into my eyes and squeezed my arm.

She never lost her smile when she whispered, "Something's bothering you."

Boy, that Agnes. There was no fooling her. I had a lousy poker face. My mind drifted from the wedding to images of Mabel lying in bed and Tom standing over her.

"Nonsense, sweetheart. It's a beautiful day, and the only thing more beautiful than the day is the bride herself. You're gorgeous," I said, and I meant it.

When we reached the altar, I hugged Agnes and gave her away and took a seat in the front pew next to Lucille. She took my hand in hers. She held a handkerchief in her other hand and dabbed at her eyes.

"I always cry at weddings," she said. "This is the first one I've been to since, well, you know."

Since the death of her husband, she meant.

The ceremony went well. I had to admit, Percival Gillman looked smashing in a tuxedo, tall, slender and distinguished with Agnes by his side. Together they made a handsome couple. Agnes's sister and a friend from church stood next to Agnes. Percival's brother was best man, and a college fraternity brother served as a groomsman.

The preacher read a couple of Bible verses, and the couple recited their vows. Percival's fraternity brother stepped forward and sang "The Very Thought of You" to piano accompaniment, and a final prayer ended the ceremony. The groom kissed the bride, and the couple walked down the aisle together. The wedding was traditional, elegant, and intimate just as Agnes had hoped it would be.

The twosome disappeared while the guests moved outside and lined the walk. Moments later, the newlyweds exited the church beneath a shower of rice. Cars were lined up along the curb. My roadster was first in line. Percival Gillman's car came next bearing a sign that read, "Just Married," and towing empty tin cans tied to the rear bumper. The other cars in the party followed.

"Here we go!" I said, and Lucille and I hopped in the roadster.

We tooted our horns and waved at folks and made fools of ourselves as we wound through downtown. On Douglas we rode east until we came to Hillside where we turned north and drove until we reached the edge of town and the Shadowlands Dance Club, operated by bandleader, Gage Brewer. Brewer made history some five years earlier by being the first musician to play the electric guitar in a live performance. His orchestra played several cheek-to-cheek numbers in honor of the wedding guests, and Lucille and I swayed together through each one.

The wedding reception was my treat. I had hastily made reservations at the dance club the day before. We made our way to a cluster of tables reserved for the "Gillman Wedding." A tiered cake decorated one of the tables, and guests added gifts to the table as they arrived.

"Pete, this is really beautiful," Agnes said, "but you're not fooling me for a minute. You hadn't planned on having this party here, did you? Something's happened that you're not telling me."

"Don't be so analytical," I said. "Quit being a detective. Enjoy your day. This is special, and so are you."

The bride and groom cut the cake, and we enjoyed refreshments and danced. The couple opened their gifts. Lucille and I gave the couple a wedding clock mounted on a cherry base with a brass plate that bore their names, Percival and Agnes Gillman, and the date, October 24, 1937. Other guests gave items for the home they would make together. The party lasted into the late afternoon until Agnes's sister said it was time to leave for Salina. She hugged Agnes and wished the couple luck and happiness, and the remaining guests did the same. Agnes whispered something to Percival who nodded and asked Lucille for a last dance. Agnes took my hand and led me to the dance floor. I held her as the orchestra played "Love is the Sweetest Thing."

"Everything is wonderful," she said. "You've helped make this day special. Thank you so much for this reception, Pete. Percival and I are both grateful."

"Hey, it isn't every day that a fella gives away his best girl," I said. "I hope you'll both be very happy."

"Thank you. Now, don't take this the wrong way. This party is lovely. You said you wanted to give me a reception, and I appreciate it, but you're not fooling me for a minute. I thought we'd be celebrating at Tom's Inn this afternoon, and I think you did, too. What happened? Did you and Tom have a falling out? Why the sudden change in plans?"

"Can't we just drop it?" I said. "I thought this would be a nice place and we could enjoy dancing to the music."

"It is nice. Everyone had a swell time, but something is wrong. Something is on your mind. You know you can't hide anything from me. Give, buster."

I held Agnes, and we did a turn or two before I spoke.

"It's Mabel," I said.

I gave Agnes a brief outline that covered Friday night's events, Mabel's stroke and her admission to the hospital.

"The doctors are encouraging," I said.

Agnes stopped dancing in the middle of the number and gave me a look and shook her head. Percival and Lucille also stopped dancing and looked at us with puzzled expressions.

"Let's go," Agnes said.

We loaded the gifts and the remains of the cake into both cars and drove across town to the Wichita Hospital and School for Nurses. On the way, I brought Lucille up-to-date on Mabel's condition.

"I didn't want to ruin the wedding," I said. "I was going to tell Agnes and you about Mabel's stroke, but I wanted to wait until this day was over."

Lucille nodded and kissed my cheek.

"I understand," she said.

The nurses were flustered at all of us descending on Mabel at once, but it was the first time I'd seen Tom smile since Friday night. Tom hugged Agnes and Lucille, and Agnes introduced him to her new husband, and they shook hands.

"Mabel has been resting well," Tom said. "She's so tired. I think she's been exhausted for some time now. The doctor wants to keep her here for a week until he is sure she is rested and her blood pressure stays down. That's fine by me."

The nurses gave us stern looks and shushed us when we got too loud, but they relented a bit when Percival went out to his car and returned with cake for everyone. Plates and forks appeared, and we all shared in the treat. A nurse came out of Mabel's room and said she was awake, so one by one we went in to wish her a speedy recovery. She looked tired and struggled to speak, but we were all happy and relieved to still have her with us.

After our visit, we gathered outside of the hospital. Lucille and I hugged the newlyweds and wished them a good time. Agnes was scheduled to return to work after a weeklong honeymoon.

For the next few days, I went to the office as usual, but I spent little time there. It seemed barren without Agnes behind her desk. I visited the university campus to learn more about the Halloween party scheduled for that upcoming Saturday night.

"It'll be well attended," Ethan Alexander assured me. "The dean has encouraged faculty to attend which means woe betide the educator who opts out of the party. I'll be there, as will my colleagues in the department—in costume—as a literary character. Care to wager on who I will be?"

I hesitated and tried to recall a literary character in a wheelchair. He let me off the hook.

"Too late. I'm going as King Richard III. Nothing to the costume, really. I'll just decorate the wheelchair as a throne, don a crown and throw on a cape. I've borrowed a pair of crutches to place beside my throne. Once I'm situated in my corner of the domain, I'll slump as if my spine is crooked and reign over the proceedings in a most regal manner."

He laughed at himself, and I joined in.

I spent time with Tom at the hospital each day and spelled him from time to time so he could grab a bite to eat. He sat next to Mabel's bed each evening until about midnight. There wasn't much he could do for her, but there was no other place he wanted to be. He never even mentioned his tavern. After she fell asleep, he went home to get some rest and returned the next morning to do it all over again.

It was midweek, and I sat with Mabel while Tom went out for a sandwich. He returned and saw her sitting up in bed, and he smiled.

I said my goodnights and was leaving the room when I heard Tom speak to Mabel.

"You know, if we weren't married, I'd ask you," he said.

Mabel's voice was weak, but I could hear her words.

"And I'd say yes," she said.

I left the hospital and chanced to drive by Tom's Inn. I was surprised to see the lights burning. I pulled over to the curb, and someone came out the door. A gentleman was leaving the inn, but he held the door so a man escorting a woman could enter. The place was obviously open for business. I got out of the roadster and went inside myself.

"Welcome, stranger. It's about time you showed up."

My mouth fell open. I took a stool, and the bartender placed a tall, cold Storz beer in front of me. The place was busy. Folks sat at tables and booths enjoying the evening.

"What's the matter, buddy. Cat got your tongue?"

I lifted the glass and swallowed some beer.

"I guess it does. What is this?" I said.

"What do you mean, what is this? This is a tavern, and what you have in your hand is a glass of beer. Don't tell me this is your first time in a bar. I wouldn't believe you."

She was having fun with me, and who could blame her?

"Agnes, I thought you were miles away on your honeymoon. What are you doing here?"

"I'm running a bar, dummy. What does it look like?"

"But what about your honeymoon?"

"No one said I couldn't run a bar on my honeymoon, did they? It's my honeymoon. I can do what I want."

"Where's Percival?"

"He just left for home. He had a beer and a bite to eat. He went back to work at the bank this week. They've rescheduled his vacation. We'll take it later."

"He had a beer and a bite to eat?" I said. "You mean you're running the kitchen, too?"

"Don't be silly. I've got all I can do to keep the beer flowing."

Agnes turned toward the kitchen.

"Hey, cookie," she said. "Come on out. There's a gent here who looks a little peckish. He needs a meal."

A figure appeared in the doorway, and my jaw dropped for the second time.

"Lucille!"

Lucille came over and hugged me and kissed me.

"I've been wondering when you would show up."

"I don't believe it," I said. "When did you two come up with this idea? How long have you been working here?"

"We opened Monday," Agnes said. "It's just for this week, at least it is for me. We worked it out with Tom last Sunday at the hospital. You were visiting Mabel in her room at the time. Tom will be back on the stick next week after Mabel is released. We'll have to wait and see about her coming back."

"If you two aren't something," I said.

"Hey, I told you I wanted a job," Lucille said. "I've been aching to get out of the house. Turns out, I like working in a kitchen. I hope Mabel returns as soon as she can, but until then, I'll keep the fires burning in the back."

"Customers haven't been complaining," Agnes said, "and the food is good. How about some chow?"

Lucille went into the kitchen and returned a few moments later with a sirloin steak on a platter next to potato salad and warm rolls. I sliced into the pink, juicy meat and took a bite. It was delicious. Agnes kept my glass full, and Lucille sat next to me at the bar and chatted and smiled at every yum I made.

He Was Dressed as Jack the Ripper

He Was Dressed as Jack the Ripper

The entire city celebrated Halloween on Saturday, and the weather cooperated by providing a warm and mild evening. Several parties were planned with the intent of entertaining youngsters while keeping them out of trouble. The city police took out a full-page advertisement in the Eagle urging citizens to remain vigilant and help stop anticipated vandalism.

The newspaper reported that the Lions Club was holding a Halloween dance in the Rose Room of the Forum on South Water Street for young people of high school and college ages. Staff and personalities from KFH radio station would be on hand to broadcast the festivities, and there would be drawings throughout the evening for prizes. Sedgwick County provided vans to shuttle the young party-goers, and the paper listed several intersections where pick-ups would be made.

The Metro Club announced a party for families of all ages to be held at Lawrence Stadium. Parents could watch their children from the stadium seats while little ones enjoyed entertainment and games on the field. This party would also have drawings and prizes with the grand prize being a shiny, green Schwinn bicycle.

Lucille and I had talked earlier in the week, and I mentioned the party. She expected me to take her out on Saturday night, and I wanted her to know that I had to work.

"I have to attend the party on campus Saturday night," I said. "I'm sorry I can't be with you, but I'll make it up to you next Saturday. Dinner and a movie?"

She smiled and agreed.

"What are you going to do at the party?" she said.

"I'll wear a costume to disguise my identity so I can observe the crowd without arousing suspicion. Professors and students from the English Department will be dressed as literary characters."

"Literary characters, huh? Sounds like fun," she said. "Who will you be?"

"I haven't decided yet. I'll pick up a mask at Woolworths."

"Oh, that's lousy," she said. "You can do better than that. Stop by my place on Saturday. I'll fix up a costume for you that will hide your identity and lend you character."

When Saturday arrived, I stopped by Lucille's house early in the evening, and she led me into the kitchen where she had placed a drawer full of makeup on the table. She left the room while I stripped to my skivvies and undershirt, then she seated me at the table. She draped a towel over my shoulders and went to work. She mussed up my hair and applied a concoction of makeup and shoe polish to dirty my face and arms and the backs of my hands. Then she handed me a set of crooked false teeth.

"Where did you get these?" I said.

"Woolworths," she said and grinned.

I popped the teeth into my mouth, and she handed me a mirror. My own mother wouldn't have recognized me.

"I look hideous," I said. "This is perfect."

"Wait a minute," she said and handed me what looked like a large, brown blanket. "Put this on."

She left the room again, and I stood to wrap myself in the blanket. I saw that there was a large hole in the middle for my head, and she had sewn a pillow into the underside of the costume near the hole. I slipped it over my head and became a hunchback, an ugly, frightening hunchback. A sash fell to the floor. I picked it up and tied it around my waist to complete the look.

Lucille came back into the kitchen and whistled.

"Now that's what I call a costume," she said.

I took a look at her and returned the whistle. She wore a white, off-the-shoulder blouse and a red, high-waist skirt. She carried a tambourine and wore gold bracelets and loop earrings, along with a gold necklace and rings on her fingers. She had a rose stuck in her hair. She looked stunning.

"Esmeralda," I said.

"Well, I'm too blonde to be an authentic gypsy, but yes, why not? What's the Hunchback of Notre Dame without his Esmeralda?"

Just like that, the hunchback had a date to the party. We left her place and drove slowly and watched for little urchins in the streets. Trick-or-treaters ran down the sidewalks from house to house. Older kids scurried in the shadows and teased and taunted the younger ones.

The Commons Building on the Wichita University campus was lit up and decorated. Music reached us from inside. People filed into the building in small groups. A few wore finery, tuxedoes and ball gowns, but most wore traditional costumes of witches, ghouls, and ghosts. Others were dressed as literary characters. A figure I recognized approached on the walk. I stepped behind him and took ahold of the handles on his wheelchair.

"Allow me, your highness," I said.

Ethan Alexander turned his head and looked up into my face and burst into laughter. His crown slipped a bit, and he straightened it with one hand and continued laughing.

"Well, I recognize the voice, but your costume sure fooled me. You look ghastly—and marvelous. Good evening, Pete."

I introduced Ethan to Lucille. Ethan looked from Lucille to me and back again and nodded knowingly.

"Ah, so we are visited by the ghosts of Victor Hugo. Well done, both of you. You've captured the spirit of the evening. Congratulations. I do have one question, though. This is a student/faculty mixer. Are you crashing the party?"

"Yes, we are," I said.

I gave Ethan a brief explanation of why we were there and the need to remain incognito.

"Well, this is exciting," he said. "I thought this would be just another dreary old assemblage, but the thought of an undercover detective working the crowd is stimulating. Of course, you can count on me to remain discrete. Now, let us away. Adventure calls."

I pushed Ethan up the walk toward the Commons and he directed me to a side entrance that had a ramp used for deliveries. When we got him inside the building and situated in his domain, as he referred to it, he pulled his canes from under his robe and assumed a slumped pose on his throne.

"You make a believable Richard III," I said.

He gave us a wry grin and wished us luck. The crowd grew larger, and the costumes added color to the streamers and balloons hanging in black and orange from the ceiling. A band made up of student musicians played a lively mixture of jazz, swing, and other contemporary tunes. Two vocalists, one male and the other female, took turns at the microphone and sang popular songs made famous by Bing Crosby, Ethel Waters, Fred Astaire, Mildred Bailey, and others. Faculty and student couples alike took to the dance floor.

Lucille and I strolled through the crowd and tried to identify costumes, especially those of literary characters. Little Bo-Peep led her date on a leash, a good sport dressed as a sheep. At least three Frankenstein monsters roamed the floor on locked-kneed stiff legs. Little Red Riding Hood made an appearance as did the Big Bad Wolf. Tom Sawyer, Becky Thatcher, and Huck Finn were present along with characters from the novels of Jane Austen and Charles Dickens.

I recognized Dr. Landis who wore a long, dark coat and a fedora pulled low over his eyes. I didn't make the costume connection until I noticed something shiny protruding from his pocket, a stick perhaps, wrapped in tin foil to look like a dagger. He was dressed as Jack the Ripper. If he was the killer I was pursuing, he was certainly dressed appropriately, but would a murderer who stabbed his victims wear such an obvious costume to a Halloween party? I pondered the question.

The characters I wanted to locate didn't arrive until the party was in full swing. A murmur rose in the crowd, and a beautiful woman turned heads. Muriel Fallon made her entrance on the arm of her husband. At first I was surprised at the couple's choice of costumes. They were in period dress of the mid-nineteenth century, southern aristocrats fresh off the plantation, from the pages of a contemporary novel, Margaret Mitchell's *Gone with the Wind*. Their choice of costumes undoubtedly fell to Mrs. Fallon. As a stunning southern lady, she captured the room in her lace and feather-fringed evening gown and emerald jewels. Lucille watched me watch Muriel cross the floor and elbowed me in the ribs.

"Easy, hunchback," she said. "You're way too ugly to capture her imagination."

"I'm not interested," I said. "Strictly business. Besides, it's her escort I care about."

Wil Fallon made a handsome plantation owner. I studied his costume and froze. He wore long gray whiskers, and he had a black top hat. Under a dark coat he wore a red checkered vest with a gold chain draped across it. As usual, every hair was in place. He was dressed exactly like grandma's great uncle, Horace. A chill swept over me as I recalled my dream from a few weeks earlier.

"What's wrong, dear?" Lucille said. "Even with all that makeup, you look like you've seen a ghost."

"I believe I have," I said.

The couple nodded and spoke to several people, mostly colleagues, I suspected, before taking a spin on the dance floor.

Now that I had spotted the couple and felt I could keep them in sight, I asked Lucille to dance. Several people smiled and made remarks on our costumes. We danced to a couple of songs. I held Lucille and thanked her for being there with me.

"I'm not very good company," I said. "I hope you know it has nothing to do with you."

"I know that," she said. "Tell me what you can about this case. I want to help."

"Every clue points to Wil Fallon as the murderer. He's the only person I've uncovered who had connections to both of the victims. No one I've spoken to thinks he is capable of murder. I have doubts about his wife, Muriel, too. She is a greedy woman, and she may want him out of the way, but I don't think she is resourceful enough to have committed two murders."

I recalled the message written in Rosemary Joy's diary:

"From one's corpus
Spirit doth cleave,
Swallowed by shadows
On All Hallows' Eve."

"Something is going to happen tonight," I said, "something bad, unless I—we can stop it. Help me keep an eye on our southern aristocrats tonight."

Fallon danced with his wife and chatted with colleagues, most of whom I didn't know. When Fallon and his wife separated to talk to other people, I asked Lucille to keep an eye on Muriel while I followed Wil. I watched him visit with Ethan Alexander, and Ethan to his credit never glanced my way while they talked. Fallon also spoke to Dr. Landis. At one point their conversation looked animated, as if they were arguing, but it may have been my imagination. I couldn't believe that their disagreements over the curriculum hadn't been settled. Eventually, Wil and Muriel came together again.

"That woman is an incurable flirt," Lucille said. "I spotted her making eyes at every man who spoke to her, and more than a few spoke to her. One man danced with her."

"Which man?" I said.

She scanned the crowd until she spotted him.

"Over there. The one wearing two faces."

The man in question was dressed in a suit and a top hat, but he wore a grotesque mask over his face. On the back of his head, he wore another mask with the face of an ordinary looking fellow.

"Dr. Jekyll and Mr. Hyde," I said.

The hour grew late, and I began to wonder if anything unusual would happen at the party. The message in the diary never mentioned the party, only All Hallows' Eve. Maybe I wasn't even in the right place. The killer could be anywhere—in or out of Wichita. Across the floor, Muriel entertained several men with her laughter and charms. She played the role of a southern lady well, straight off the pages of the novel. I looked for Wil Fallon but didn't spot him.

"Do you see Fallon?" I said to Lucille.

"He was there a moment ago," she said.

We circled the dancers and moved across the floor toward the cluster of faculty members. I still didn't see Fallon and felt a sense of unease. Behind the guests, a set of stairs rose to the upper floor. I had noticed some traffic on the steps earlier in the evening, and when we got to the top I saw why. Down a hallway, we found additional restrooms, and beyond the restrooms another set of stairs led back down to the ballroom. I caught a glimpse of a figure going down those stairs but couldn't make out who it was.

"Wait here," I said and stepped into the men's room. It was empty except for the body on the floor beneath the sink. Staring up and seeing nothing were the open eyes of Dr. Sherman Landis, aka Jack the Ripper. The sink was plugged, and water ran over its edge and onto the body. I turned off the water and checked for a pulse I knew I wouldn't find. A knife, similar to the ones found in the bodies of the previous victims, protruded from the base of Landis's skull. It had been driven into the back of his neck and up toward the brain. An equilateral triangle was embossed on the handle of the knife. Like the knife found in the boy's body in the county, this triangle had no line running through it, but it was pointed downward instead of up.

I noticed a slip of paper sticking out of a coat pocket and used a paper towel over my fingers to remove it. The poem written on it was familiar. It was the final line of Edgar Allan Poe's "The Raven."

"And my soul from out that shadow that lies floating on the floor

Shall be lifted—nevermore!"

You're Going to be Killed
You're Going to be Killed

We heard sirens in the distance when we got into the roadster.

"The cops will be questioning people all night," I said. "I don't want to be here for that. Let's go."

Someone must have called the police before I discovered the body. It may have been the killer himself. We drove around the backside of campus to avoid police cars headed for the Commons Building. I circled toward an exit near the Liberal Arts Building and noticed a faint glow coming from one of the second floor windows. I turned the lights off on the car and rolled to a stop.

"Someone's inside, and I think I know who it is," I said. "Wait here."

"Oh, you're not leaving me alone in the dark with a killer loose on campus," Lucille said. "I'm coming with you."

I couldn't blame her. We went to the building entrance and found the door unlocked. Our eyes took a moment to adjust to the dim lighting that filtered in from streetlights outside. We climbed the stairs and saw light coming from Room 205. I stuck my head into the doorway and saw Fallon bent over his desk holding a sheet of paper in one hand and his head in the other. I wondered if he'd been weeping. He sensed my presence and looked up. His mouth fell open, and he spoke.

"My god, what is this? Are you the one? Are you the killer? Who are you? What are you doing here?"

I forgot I was still wearing my costume and looked like a monstrous hunchback. Fallon assumed the murderer had come to pay him a visit.

"I was just about to ask you the same question," I said.

"I know that voice. You're Pete Stone. What are you doing here? Who's that with you?"

Lucille came in behind me. I made the introductions. Lucille took a seat next to me.

"There's been another murder," Fallon said. "Dear Sherman Landis, my colleague, my friend. Stabbed in the back of the head. I've called the police, and I have to get back. Muriel will be wondering where I've gone."

If Fallon was the killer and only playacting, he was good at it. He seemed genuinely shaken and distraught. I turned to Lucille who seemed focused on everything she heard.

"I saw you speak to Dr. Landis earlier this evening," I said. "I thought maybe your conversation was heated."

"That was nothing. Sherman and I often disagreed on things here in the department, class schedules, curriculum, faculty publications or whatever. We laughed about it often. Our conflicts worked to keep the English department from becoming stagnant. Nothing signals a decline in fresh ideas like having a faculty that always agrees with each other. Intellectual give and take is necessary to growth and progress."

"Why did you leave the Commons Building?" I said. "Why are you here in your office?"

"The knife. I saw that horrible knife," he said. "Tell me, the other deaths. Were those people stabbed with similar weapons?"

I assured him that they were. He looked down and shook his head and handed me the paper he had been reading. There were illustrations on the paper of four equilateral triangles, each with an accompanying explanation of how they represented physical elements. The first triangle was pointed upward and represented fire. The second also pointed upward but was bisected by a horizontal line. It represented air. The next triangle pointed downward and represented water. A fourth triangle also pointed downward. It was bisected by a horizontal line and represented earth.

"What is this?" I said. "Where did you get this?"

"This is part of my research, a page to be added to a paper I'm writing on Greek influences in Shakespeare's work."

"Shakespeare and the Four Humors."

"That's right. How did you know?"

"I've seen it lying on your desk."

He reached into a drawer and withdrew the manuscript.

"I confess I scanned your paper," I said, "the day you left me in your office and invited me to read something while I waited. Reading it led me to believe that you knew more about these crimes than you've been letting on. The clues point to your guilt. The first two victims were unknown to each other, but they did have something in common. Each was a recipient of your generosity. You gave money to each of them and their families. That leaves Dr. Landis. Did you give money to him?"

"No, not really," he said. "I did make a loan to him several months ago so he could make a down payment on some real estate, but that was strictly a loan, not a gift. He intended to pay that money back, and the man's word was good."

I glanced over Fallon's shoulder at a wall calendar displaying the days of the month, October. I studied the dates and noted a circle around the current day, October 30th, with the words, "Faculty/Student Party," written within the circle. I pondered the days of the weeks and their dates and something hit me. The crimes, the coincidences, the methods of murder. What diabolical mind had conceived such a plan? A pattern came clear.

"May I see your manuscript?" I said.

I turned to the pages on the four bodily humors, sanguine, choleric, phlegmatic, and melancholic and read the characteristics of each. Sanguine behavior signified a young person, a person such as Rosemary Joy Cleveland. Its body part was the heart, and its element was air. Rosemary Joy Cleveland was stabbed in the chest with a knife bearing the symbol for air, a bisected triangle pointed up. Her body was found beneath a ceiling fan that had been running, furnishing air. The killer had made certain that her body would lie at that particular spot, a sordid, symbolic gesture.

Choleric behavior signified childhood, and its body part was the gall bladder. The knife in Andrew Egan, the young boy in the country, was thrust to his midsection, toward the gall bladder. It bore the symbol for fire on its handle, an upward pointed triangle. Fire was also the element for choleric. The killer had stoked the campfire and burned all of the firewood that night, another symbolic act.

Phlegmatic represented maturity and the brain. Its physical element was water. Dr. Landis had been murdered with a knife to the base of his skull that entered his brain. Water from the sink flowed onto his body, and, of course, the knife was marked with the symbol for water, a downward pointed triangle.

I read the details of each humor aloud to Fallon and Lucille who listened without interrupting and explained how each in turn applied to the three victims. However, there were four humors outlined in Fallon's paper and only three victims. The fourth humor was melancholic, and it represented old age. I looked at Fallon. He wore a false gray beard, but his natural hair color was snowy white. The poetry planted on the corpses was an added touch pointing to someone familiar with literature, someone like an English professor.

"It's you," I said to Fallon.

"Me? You can't possibly believe I'm responsible for this. I'm no criminal. I'm as stunned by all of this as you are."

"It's been you all along," I said. "The others were simply minor characters in a grander play, a tragedy with you in the leading role. This has all been carefully staged and enacted by an evil and intelligent mind."

"Now, stop this, Stone. I must insist."

"Relax, professor. You're not the murderer," I said.

"But, you said it was me. What did you mean by that?"

"You are the fourth bodily humor, the fourth victim. It's to be you."

Lucille gasped, and Fallon sank back in his chair.

"Me?" he said.

"This must be stopped," Lucille said. It was the first time she'd spoken since meeting Fallon. "Pete, you've got to do something."

"You know who it is, don't you?" Fallon said. "You know who the killer is. Well, tell us. Who is it? Where is he?"

"I don't know where he is at the moment, but I know where he's going to be, and I know when he'll be there. Lucille pointed him out to me earlier this evening."

She leaned toward me and squeezed my arm.

"I did? When did I do that? Who is it?"

I smiled at Lucille and turned back toward Fallon.

"He was at the party in costume. Your wife, Muriel, danced with him this evening before he murdered your colleague. Earlier I wondered if Dr. Landis might be the killer. I was intrigued by his Jack the Ripper costume, a villain who stabbed his victims. I also figured Landis would know you as well as anyone on campus and could stage the crimes to make you appear to be guilty. Now I know the killer is Dr. Jekyll and Mr. Hyde, a man with two sides, one honest and one evil, and he's going to keep his promise. He's going to murder you tomorrow night on All Hallows' Eve."

♦♦♦

Sunday Night was All Hallows' Eve

Muriel carried a book and a cup of tea and retired to her bedroom upstairs. How involved was she in the murders? Was she involved at all? The answers to those questions remained unclear. Fallon told her that we had business to discuss and he'd be along after we finished. He assured me that there was no phone on the second floor. I didn't want her making any calls. After Muriel retired, I adjusted the lighting on the lower floor of the house. The front room was unlit, but a nightlight burned at the bottom of the stairs and cast shadows onto the walls. Fallon and I waited in his study down the hall with the door opened. The lights in the study were dimmed, also. We waited in the shadows, but I didn't anticipate a long wait.

It was Sunday night, the night after the university Halloween party, and the last night of October, the thirty-first, All Hallows' Eve. The university, along with the entire city, had celebrated Halloween a day early that year, on Saturday the thirtieth, rather than hold their festivities on Sunday night, the actual All Hallows' Eve.

The date came to me when I noticed the calendar in Fallon's office. The killer referred to All Hallows' Eve when he wrote his rhyme in Rosemary Joy's diary, "Swallowed by shadows, on All Hallows' Eve." I had mistakenly assumed All Hallows' Eve meant

Saturday night, but Sunday night was the night in question. Sunday night was All Hallows' Eve.

We heard sounds from beyond the kitchen, the sounds of a door at the rear of the house opening and closing. Fallon had locked the backdoor, but neither of us were surprised when it opened so easily. The killer had visited the Fallon home on other occasions and obviously carried a key. The backdoor is where he had exited the house when I visited Muriel. He'd gone out that door and lain in wait in the bushes before knocking me unconscious. In his haste to leave, he'd neglected to take his burning cigarette out of the ashtray, the cigarette Muriel crushed out. Fallon had told me the truth. Smoke irritated her sinuses.

In the dim light, the figure cast a shadow when he entered the front room. He moved like a ghost toward the base of the stairs. I tensed and started to move and recalled my grandmother's advice, "Just wait and watch. Slow down. Go easy."

I eased down the hallway with my Smith & Wesson .38 at my side. He placed a foot on the bottom step, and I moved out of the hallway with my gun extended.

"Hold it," I said.

The nightlight shone bright enough for him to see me. He looked at my face and looked at my gun. He remained silent, just as he had when I saw him last. His shoulders slumped.

"Good evening, Arthur," I said. "Shall I call you Arthur or do you prefer Dr. Jekyll or Mr. Hyde? You'd better sit down."

Fallon switched on the lights and entered the room behind me. Arthur Cross looked from me to Fallon and back at me. He hung his head and dropped into a chair. Muriel must have heard our voices. She came down the stairs. Arthur watched her every move.

"That was you last night dressed as Jekyll and Hyde wasn't it?" I said.

He nodded.

"I have to compliment you. The characters you chose are a perfect fit for your dual personality."

"What is this?" Muriel said. "What's going on? Arthur, what are you doing here? Wil?"

"Please sit down, Muriel," Fallon said.

Muriel took a seat on the sofa, and her husband sat down next to her. I was the only person left standing. I was also the only person holding a gun. I kept it pointed at Cross.

"It's warm tonight, and you're wearing gloves," I said.

Arthur looked down at his hands and forced a smile.

"I think you know why I'm wearing gloves," he said.

"Yes, I think I do," I said. "Very slowly now, take that knife out of your pocket and place it on the table."

He moved slowly and did what I told him. His hands were shaking. I picked up the knife and saw a bisected downward triangle on its handle, the symbol for the fourth element, earth. I put it in my coat pocket.

"Arthur, how could you kill those innocent people?" Fallon said. "Why? Why would you do such a thing? And why do you want to kill me?"

Arthur stared at Muriel and she returned his look, then looked down and shook her head. He said nothing.

"Do you have anything to add, Muriel?" Fallon said.

Muriel leaned forward.

"Arthur, please say something," she said. "Is this true? Did you kill those people?"

Arthur sat in silence for a long moment before he spoke.

"I did it for you, Muriel. I did it for us. Those people, they were taking your money. You said so. That's what you told me. I wanted them to stop. I wanted you to have that money. I wanted you to be happy. I wanted to make you happy. I wanted . . ., I wanted you, Muriel. I wanted you, and I wanted you to want me. I thought with your husband out of the way . . ."

His voice trailed off. Arthur Cross bent his head and sobbed into his hands. I found a telephone and called the police.

I wondered that night as I would wonder even later if Muriel Fallon shared in Arthur Cross's guilt. Cross had thrust the knives into his victims, not Muriel Fallon, but there was no question that her flirtations with a vulnerable, young man had prompted his behavior. Flirtations alone did not make her guilty, but had there been more than flirting? Had Muriel and Arthur engaged in an affair? Those were questions that would remain unanswered. The professor was intelligent enough to decide if he and his wife needed to discuss their relationship between themselves.

I recalled the notations Rosemary Joy had made in her diary. Had she puzzled over Muriel's intentions also? Her entries, "My Faith? My Friend? MF?" Was MF a reference to Muriel Fallon? I considered Rosemary Joy's final gesture as she lay dying. She'd clutched her necklace, the chain and cross she received as a little girl for perfect attendance in Sunday school. Had clutching her cross been a final act of faith or a clue to the name of her killer, Arthur Cross?

Arthur Cross would pay for his actions. Only an evil mind and a person of low character would devise and carry out such cruel murders. The police would get him to open up and explain his motives in detail. Muriel had voiced her concerns about money to Cross just as she had with me. Muriel knew where her husband's money went, those people to whom Fallon had felt protective. She gave the names of those people to a young man infatuated by her charms. Cross was smitten by the attentions of a beautiful, more experienced woman. As a grand gesture, Cross created his scheme, planting clues that pointed to Dr. Fallon along the way. He probably assumed that with Fallon out of the way, whether murdered or in prison, Muriel would belong to him. Cross was so naïve, as if a woman like Muriel Fallon would ever give herself to a boy. She probably thought of him as no more than a puppy or a toy, a puppet on a string. He was too unaware to play ball in the big leagues.

A recollection of my conversation with Fallon's other graduate student, Cynthia Buckman, cleared up the connection between the details of the murders and the themes in Fallon's manuscript. The text of "Shakespeare and the Four Humors" suggested that its author must be the killer, or, if not the author, someone familiar with the manuscript. When I talked to Cynthia, she said that graduate students often helped their mentors with their research and even typed some of their work. Arthur Cross had read Fallon's work and was familiar with the contents of his manuscript. Cross used that knowledge in plotting his crimes.

Cynthia must have known about Cross's infatuation with Muriel Fallon. What had she said to me that day in their office? "Alas, poor Yorick pines for another, an unrequited love, I'm afraid." Arthur Cross wouldn't pine for long, I thought. Only long enough to be tried, convicted, and executed.

On Monday, the day after Arthur Cross's arrest, I sat in Lieutenant McCormick's office and endured the verbal tongue lashing he had prepared for me and that I probably deserved.

"You promised you'd share everything you had with the police," he said.

"I've shared everything," I said. "I've given you all the evidence I've uncovered."

"What about his?" he said and held up the diary. "When did you uncover this?"

"Recently," I said.

I gave the diary to McCormick, but only after securing his promise that he would return it to me after Cross's trial. I wanted to pass it along to Henry Brown. Brown deserved to possess the copy of his sister's final thoughts.

McCormick made me repeat everything that had happened, everything I knew about the case over and over until we both grew tired of looking at each other, of breathing the same air in the same room with one another. He finally relented. He was angry with me, but he'd get over it. He was often angry with me. He never stayed angry for long. The killer was behind bars, and the case was closed. That was the most important thing. No matter how many times Mac and I danced our dance together, justice took center stage. I stood up and handed McCormick a cigar.

"Made in the Dominican Republic by the Leon Family," I said. "A gift from a grateful client."

McCormick muttered something that may have been thanks and bit the end off of the cigar. He lit a match and leaned back in his chair. I left.

So, That's Exactly What I Did
So, That's Exactly What I Did

As always, Mother Nature kept her own calendar, and when November arrived, she brought north winds and cooler temperatures along with it. The university cancelled classes on Wednesday afternoon so those who wished could attend a memorial service in the auditorium in honor of Dr. Sherman Landis. Students and faculty leaned into the wind and held the fronts of their wraps closed against the cold. No matter how long we Kansans lived on the plains, sudden changes in the weather caught us by surprise.

After the service, I visited Dr. Fallon in his office and offered condolences on the loss of his friend and colleague.

"Thank you," he said. "So much waste, so many lives taken from us. It's all so painful. When I first called you, I had no idea it would lead to this, to all of these deaths."

"No one owns a crystal ball, professor. Don't be too hard on yourself. You did what you could. The culprit is behind bars, and we can be thankful that you're still alive."

There was a knock at the door. I glanced at my watch as Fallon started to rise from his chair.

"Let me get this," I said.

Fallon wore a puzzled expression when I opened the door and said, "Come in."

Ralph Waldo entered followed by Henry Brown. Brown shifted from foot to foot and scanned the office while Ralph and Fallon shook hands.

"Henry, I'd like you to meet this gentleman. His name is Wil Fallon."

Fallon came from around his desk with a smile on his face. He took Henry's hand in both of his and shook it.

"I'm so very happy to meet you, Henry," he said and turned toward me. "This is such a wonderful surprise. I'm grateful to you. Maybe something good will come out of all of this after all. Thank you."

We shook hands, and I touched the brim of my hat.

"We'll be running along," I said.

Ralph and I turned to leave, and as I closed the door, I heard Fallon speak.

"Sit down, Henry. We have a lot to talk about."

I crossed over the threshold, and a voice boomed, "It's about time you showed up, gumshoe. I was beginning to think you'd forgotten your friends."

Tom placed a glass of Storz beer on the bar and reached for my hand.

"It's good to see you back where you belong," I said, "behind the bar working the stick."

"It's good to see you on a barstool, too."

"How's Mabel? I hope she's doing well."

"Mabel is fussy, and she's ornery, and she's crabby. That's how she is."

Then he grinned.

"But she's alive and back home with me, and I couldn't be happier. She fusses because she wants to come back to work, but she knows she has to rest. She has a lot of recovering to do. It'll take time, but the old gal will make it. Pete, we'd have never gotten through this without you. Mabel knows that, too. I hope you know how much we appreciate it. Those visits at the hospital meant the world to us."

I sipped my beer and waved the back of my hand.

"I didn't do anything you wouldn't have done for me. Others did more than I did."

Tom shook his head and chuckled.

"Do you believe those gals?" he said. "That Agnes and Lucille just about floored me. They spoke to me in the hospital. Said they wanted to run the place till I got back. They did run it, too, like they'd been tending bar for years. Business didn't drop off at all. Customers showed up just as they always had. The gals ran the bar and the kitchen. I owe them a lot."

"We both do," I said.

Agnes had returned to work that week. She hadn't had her honeymoon, but we agreed she had one coming. She and Percival decided to wait until the holidays arrived to take a trip. As for Lucille, I'd spoken to her by telephone, but I hadn't seen her since driving her home Saturday evening from the university campus. That was four nights earlier, the night of the Dr. Landis murder. After that night, I wasn't sure she'd want to see me.

A customer over my shoulder called for more beer in a too-loud voice, and Tom rolled his eyes. He came around the bar and walked over to the guy's table.

"More beer," the drunk said.

"You've had plenty to drink," Tom said. "How about a bite to eat instead?"

"Didn't ask for a bite to eat. I said I wanted a beer."

"No more beer. Tap's run dry. How about a sandwich? On the house."

"You think I'm drunk, don't ya? Not drunk. Just thirsty."

"Fine," Tom said. "I'll throw in a cup of coffee."

"Don't want . . ."

There was movement behind Tom, and the guy stopped talking mid-sentence. Lucille appeared carrying a plate of food and a steaming cup. She placed a sandwich and coffee in front of the customer and smiled.

"Here you are," she said.

He took a gander at Lucille and offered a crooked smile. He sat up straight and acted the gentleman. At least tried. He straightened a tie he wore only in his imagination, and he attempted to speak without slurring his words, but it was futile.

"Thank you, young lady," he said. "I'm very grateful."

That's what he hoped to say, but he slurred over the 'k' in thank you, and grateful sounded like grapefruit. I shook my head. The only thing more pathetic than a drunk being drunk was a drunk acting sober. Lucille left the man's table and walked toward me. I stood up from my barstool.

"Hello, Pete."

"Lucille. Well done. You handled that guy like a seasoned pro."

She shrugged.

"Can we talk?"

"Sure," I said.

She led me to a corner in the back, and we sat across from each other in a booth. A man and a woman came through the door and took a table close to the front. We were alone at the back of the barroom. Lucille reached across the table and took my hands in hers.

"I've wanted to talk to you for several days," she said. "Now, I don't know where to start."

"Take your time," I said. "I'm not going anywhere."

"The case? Is it closed?"

228

"The case is closed. The murderer has been apprehended and is behind bars."

Lucille nodded and squeezed my hands.

"So much violence," she said, "so much death. Now, it's over."

"Yes, it's over. The case is over. Violence and death will continue, however. There will be another case in the future and another after that. Crime never stops. You understand that, don't you?"

She closed her eyes and nodded.

"I love you, Lucille. I love you, and nothing can change that. It's just a fact of nature. I will always love you, and I'll go on loving you, whether we're together or not. If you are unable to accept me for who I am and what I do, that will not change my love for you. We'll be apart, and I'll respect that, but I'll still love you."

She nodded.

"I know that. That's who you are," she said. "I love you, too. I've fought my feelings for some time now, but I do love you. Only now, something has changed."

Here it comes, I thought. I feared what she'd say next.

"Saturday night, when that poor man was stabbed and killed, I couldn't bear seeing it. It was so cruel, so vicious. I wanted it all to go away. I wanted to be someplace else, away from that place, away from death."

She dabbed at her eyes with a handkerchief. I remained silent.

"Then, in the professor's office, the way you considered the evidence, the way you shuffled the pieces of the puzzle until it came together, the way you solved the crime, that's when I knew. At that moment, I realized that's who you are. That's what you do. It's what you were meant to do, and I could never ask you to change. Asking you to change who you are would only be another act of cruelty. I couldn't do that. So, I don't want you to change. I want you to keep on solving crimes. I want you to bring justice into your little corner of the world as you call it."

We looked into each other's eyes, and I waited for her to continue.

"I want you to keep right on being a detective, Pete. The only difference now is, I want you to do it with me in your life."

My eyebrows went up.

"I love you," she said, "only now I love you for who you are, not in spite of who you are. I love you for who you are and what you do, and I want you to keep on being who you are and doing what you do. I want to go on loving you and holding you, and I want you to love me and hold me, too. Hold me, Pete. Hold me and never let me go."

With Lucille's hands in mine, I stood up and moved to the other side of the booth. She stood, and I wrapped my arms around her. I wanted her. I wanted her, and she wanted me. Who knew what the future would bring? It didn't matter as long as we were together. Like I told the professor, no one owned a crystal ball. That's what made the adventure worth living. Lucille and I loved each other, and that's all that mattered. She wanted me to hold her. She wanted me to hold her and never let her go, and that's what I wanted, too.

So, that's exactly what I did.

The End

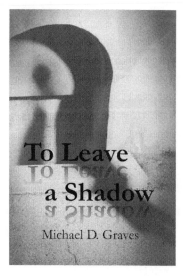

Publisher: Meadowlark - 2015
ISBN: 978-0692567791

Spring 1937

Black flies swarmed over the body, even before they got it out of the water. The buzzing, hissing swirl made a difficult job even harder. Two cops, one on each side of the bloated corpse, grunted and swore as they struggled against the river current. Each grabbed a hold under a limp arm and tugged against the powerful eddies, leaning backwards to gain leverage, fighting for purchase on the river bottom. The muddy water flowed over and around the soggy mass. They gasped for air and gagged when they sucked it in. The stench was thick and foul, the sort that lingers in your nostrils and wakes you late at night and puts you off your breakfast the next morning.

I smoked a cigarette and watched the struggle. It was humid, and I was perspiring. I took off my hat and wiped my brow with a handkerchief. My shirt stuck to my back. Rivulets of sweat trickled down my neck. I stuck a finger inside my collar and raised my head to take in some fresh air, but it was fruitless. To the south, a meat packing plant belched out rancid offal fumes. To the west, a bakery added a sticky, sweet cinnamon scent. The odors from the factories mingled beneath the heavy clouds and descended on the city below. It smelled like a fart in a pastry shop.

Somewhere in the distance a horn honked and then another. A church bell rang and tires rumbled over brick streets. Brakes squealed. A siren wailed in the distance and a plane flew overhead.

Several people stood around the perimeter, shifting from foot to foot, gawking and then looking away in disgust. Almost anyplace else in the city would have been more pleasant, but our species has an innate urge to observe the grotesque. Some watched, others covered their mouths or mumbled to companions, and someone bent over and gagged. Somebody swore softly, and somebody coughed.

The two policemen finally dragged the body ashore, and the buzz of the flies grew louder. The uniformed cops bent over at the waist with their hands on their knees gasping for air. I stared down at the swollen corpse and swallowed the bile rising in my throat. I thought about the poor bastard who once inhabited that body and pondered the fickleness of fate. Why him? What had he ever done? Why not him? Does anyone deserve to die like this?

I thought about his widow sitting at home, eager for him to return, and I wondered how she would react when she got the gruesome news. How else could she react? She'd crumble like a KO'd boxer. This guy wouldn't be coming home tonight or any other night. He'd never again come through the door, peck his wife on the cheek, and ask what's for dinner. She'd never again ask him about his day. His life was over, spent, wrung out of him by a muddy, roiling river. Life is fragile, life is futile, and we all cash in one way or another, but this guy had drawn a particularly lousy death. I looked down at the rotting mass and crushed my cigarette beneath my shoe. I continued to stare at the body for a long moment. I shook my head and asked myself for maybe the hundredth time why I'd ever gotten into this business.

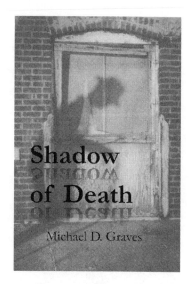

Publisher: Meadowlark - 2017
ISBN: 978-0-9966801-6-5

Saturday, June 5

The first time I met the cop we had words. You might've called it an altercation. Maybe even a fight. It was night, late at night, going into the wee hours of the morning, and I'd been drinking, again. I'd been drinking a lot lately. The cop braced me on the sidewalk down the street from Tom's Inn, planting a fleshy paw on my chest with a stiff arm. He flashed a grin that bore not a trace of good humor. He leaned in and sniffed my breath and snapped his head back.

"Ugh, man. You smell like a drunken bum. You're stink-o, you are. Who are you, buddy? What's your name?"

I fumbled through my pockets and pulled out a card.

"Pete Stone, Private Investigations," he said. "So, you're a gumshoe. Well, you're drunk, gumshoe. I hope you don't think you're going to drive your fancy automobile over my city streets in your condition. Cause if you do, you've got another think coming."

I stood under a yellow streetlight. My Jones Six Roadster, top down, was parked at the curb three steps away. My keys dangled from my fingertips. I glanced at my car. I glanced at my keys. I looked at the cop.

"Wise deduction, Sherlock," I said. I may have slurred. "How'd you figure that?"

Tom and I had spent the better part of the evening perched on barstools, swapping stories and lies, and lowering the level of a bottle of rye whiskey. We'd discussed our lives, what we'd done, what we hadn't done, what we wished we hadn't done. We'd bounced around the country's problems and agreed the solution to halting the current Depression was to boot out the politicians and replace them each year with whichever team won the World Series. We'd proclaimed that the humblest barbeque in Jerkwater, Kansas tasted better than the finest steak in Delmonico's Restaurant, never mind that neither of us had ever eaten a steak at Delmonico's or any other fine restaurant in New York City. And we'd pondered why the women we loved always broke our hearts and we kept coming back for more. It was the pondering over one woman in particular that had led me to the bottle, the barstool, and to bending the ear of my longtime pal and confidant, Tom, owner of the inn bearing his name.

Now it was late, the whiskey was gone, the inn was closed, and I was on the sidewalk, weaving on wobbly pins in front of a beat cop. I was filled to the gills with wisdom, wit, and bullet-proof courage. The cop was unimpressed.

"Okay, wise guy. Give me the keys. You're not driving anywhere."

That seemed an unreasonable request. Then again, I was in no condition to be reasonable. I puffed out my chest like an idiot and said something stupid that besmirched the cop's parentage. His eyes grew wide, and a vein bulged on his neck. His hand went for his nightstick. My arms went up, and I heard, or felt, an explosion. For an instant, it was all rockets and a light show blazing in my skull, then the lights dimmed and faded into darkness. Later, I would swear that's all I could remember. After that, however, I would be consumed with doubt.

The next time I saw the cop he lay in the morgue, stretched out on a slab. My hands were cuffed, my head throbbed, and my vision was blurry, but I could make out the third eye in the cop's forehead, the one the bullet had put there. My aching ribs made each breath an exercise in pain, and hammers clanged in my skull, but I could process a thought. I had heard the voice, I had listened to the charges, and I knew where I stood. A cop lay dead, murdered. I was found lying next to him, out cold but breathing. My .38 Smith & Wesson, with a spent cartridge, lay on the sidewalk next to me. How and why my gun came to be there was a mystery to me. I couldn't explain it. I had no memory of pulling the trigger. No one else was around, but someone had seen or heard something. Someone had made the call. I was arrested, cuffed, and tossed into jail. Maybe the arresting officers had jumped to conclusions. Maybe they hadn't. I was in no condition to argue. I was in deep trouble, and I knew it. I was booked on a murder charge. I was booked as the sole suspect in the murder of one of Wichita's finest. I was accused of killing a cop.

daveleikerphotography.com

About the Author

About the Author

Michael D. Graves created the character of Pete Stone as a memorial to his grandfather. His first Pete Stone novel, *To Leave a Shadow,* was selected as a 2016 Kansas Notable Book. *All Hallows' Shadows* is his third Pete Stone novel.

Mike's writing has appeared in *Cheap Detective Stories, Thorny Locust, Flint Hills Review,* and elsewhere. He is an author of *Green Bike, a group novel,* along with Kevin Rabas and Tracy Million Simmons. He lives with his wife in Emporia, Kansas. They are both members of the Kansas Authors Club.

When life conjures its riddles, Mike turns to back roads and baseball for answers.

Acknowledgments

Many generous people helped me write this book. Tracy Million Simmons at Meadowlark Books designed and edited the book. We've been together for years, Tracy, and your suggestions continue to make my work better. Thank you.

Dave Leiker provided the cover photos. As always, your artist's eye lends magic to my books. Thank you, Dave.

I'm grateful to several librarians, including Kathie Buckman at Emporia State University and Cynorra Jackson and Mary Nelson at Wichita State University. The information these women provided was invaluable to my story, especially a link to the 1937 edition of *Parnassus,* the yearbook of The University of Wichita. Thank you all.

Nathan Beals with Watch Works in Wichita introduced me to the history of the Wichita Watch Company. He sent the June, 1993 edition of the *NAWCC Bulletin,* a publication of the National Association of Watch and Clock Collectors, Inc., that contained a valuable article on the creation of the 1887 company and its hasty demise. Thank you, Nathan.

Monica Graves and Rick Graves read early drafts of the story and offered comments and encouragement. Thank you both.

I'm grateful for my association with the many writers in the Kansas Authors Club and Emporia Writers Group. Kevin Rabas, Tracy Million Simmons, Curtis Becker, Kerry Moyer, and Cheryl Unruh are some of the people who are always there for me and for others. Thank you all.

Some of the information on the four humors I used in this story was Courtesy of the National Library of Medicine. Thank you.

Finally, this book is dedicated to the memory of Bill Lang, brother-in-law, friend, and a pal of Pete Stone's, too. All of us who knew Bill miss his good humor and contagious laugh. He left us too suddenly and too soon.

Read
A Meadowlark Book
meadowlark-books.com

Nothing feels better than home

While we at Meadowlark Books love to travel, we also cherish our home time. We are nourished by our open prairies, our enormous skies, community, family, and friends. We are rooted in this land, and that is why Meadowlark Books publishes regional authors.

When you open one of our fiction books, you'll read delicious stories that are set in the Heartland. Settle in with a volume of poetry, and you'll remember just how much you love this place too—the landscape, its skies, the people.

Meadowlark Books publishes memoir, poetry, short stories, and novels. Read stories that began in the Heartland, that were written here. Add to your Meadowlark Book collection today.

Specializing in Books by Authors from the Heartland Since 2014

Made in the USA
Middletown, DE
09 June 2022

66887694R00149